DIAMOND MAN

Mohsen Bahonar

Somayeh Mohammadi

Title: Diamond Man

Authors: Mohsen Bahonar, Somayeh Mohammadi

ISBN: 978-1942912040

LCCN: 2015921020

Publisher: Supreme Art, Los Angeles, Ca, USA

Prepare for Publishing: Asan Nashr,

www.ASANASHR.com

On a cold night in Los Angeles, Fernanda and her husband Daniel went to a club for the rich along with their friends. An hour after their arrival, while Daniel and Fernanda were dancing, some flyers were distributed among the people at the club in which an entertaining trip to space was offered for those who were financially endowed and could sign up for it. While Fernanda and Daniel were dancing the flyer was handed to them.

Fernanda: What exhilarating news! Honey, do you think we should sign up for it?
Daniel: I have always dreamed of going on a trip like this. How about we ask if our friends would like to join us on this trip?

Fernanda: That's a great idea!
Having said that she called out to their friends and said:
Guys! We want to take a group trip to space! Would you like to come?
I would love to come! Ratin said as he turned towards his wife, Mitra, and said: How about you?

Mitra said: You know how much I love excitement .
Fernanda: Then you're in!
Then he turned to his other friends, Franco and Sofia, and asked: How about you guys?

Sofia replied: Franco and I are in too! What a great idea you guys! Since we're so close we can have lots of fun there and this will turn into an excellent and exciting trip.

Ratin: I think so too. I'm so excited.
Right that minute a man approached them and said: My friends, my name is John and I own this club. Are you guys new here? Then he recognized Fernanda and said: I'm glad to see you again after all these years. This is the best club in town.

Fernanda said: Yeah, a long time has passed since we were in university together.

John: Yeah, those were the good old days. Good for you for having chosen the best club in town, my management skills are pretty good and everybody's satisfied with the service they receive here.

Fernanda: Exactly!
Someone called for John at that moment and he was forced to leave them.
Fernanda: I do not like that guy! He's always bossing people around and trying to show off. He's a proud and egotistic aristocrat. Guys I don't think a club that such a person owns is worth going to. Let's finish our drinks and leave.

Ratin: The other club wasn't good either. We should just stop going to clubs which belong to aristocrats.

Mitra: Well, we're rich too! But we act like normal people! I don't know why money makes some people so arrogant!?

Ratin: Exactly! If you take their money from them, will they still be rich?
This was when one of the people at the club came up to Mitra and said: Hello, I'm Anna, Catherine's mom. Are you a member of this club? I've never seen you here before!

Mitra replied: No, we are a guest here, by the way how is Catherine?
Anna: She's doing good. She turned out to be very smart and is busy with school. By the way, one of my friends is looking for a Taekwondo coach for her son, could I introduce you to her?

Mitra: Of course, give her the address and phone number of the gym. When would he like to start?
Anna: I don't really know.

Mitra: It's okay. Tell her to call me tomorrow.
Anna: Thanks. Since I had told her all about you she wanted you to be her son's coach.

Mitra: Thank you.

Anna: It was nice to see you.

Mitra: You too.

Fernanda: Hey guys! Should we go?

They left the club after having said goodbye.

Fernanda: I don't know why I don't run into one of my students so I can show off.

Daniel: Don't be jealous! Remember last year and how we ran into one of your students in Canada and how he introduced you to everyone and told them you were the best Samba instructor he had had and you were forced to do all the Samba moves and everybody applauded you?

Fernanda: You're right! I forgot all about that!

Daniel: You gotta let it go!

Fernanda: Let's forget about it! Now, where to?

Ratin: Let's go to our place! We can hang out there!

Everybody agreed and since their children were in the care of nannies and baby sitters they all headed towards Ratin and Mitra's house.

Mitra called the guys and said: No talking about work and business and economics tonight!

Everybody laughed and this turned into a discussion about how men and women socialize in individual groups until this discussion finally came to an end when Fernanda said:

Okay why don't we play backgammon? Ratin, why don't you bring that Backgammon you made yourself. We wanna have fun and place bets and no one can complain, who's in?

Everyone raised their hands and they played and talked for hours until finally they all went home. The next day Fernanda said to Daniel: " How about we go back to Brazil for Christmas?"

Daniel: That's a great idea!

Fernanda: But we can't go alone!

Daniel: Of course not! We can't leave the kids alone!!!

Fernanda: No, I mean we should go with the guys! Ratin, Mitra, Sofia, and Franco.

Daniel: Ohhh, got it. That would be perfect!

Fernanda: So…why don't we call them now!

Daniel: No, they might still be asleep!

Fernanda: They have gotten enough sleep by now!

Daniel: It's the weekend! They were up all night! We'll call them in the afternoon!

It was 5pm when the phone in Ratin's home rang and Mitra picked it up. Fernanda told her all about their plan to go to Brazil for the holidays. Mitra said she'd discuss it with Ratin and get back to them. Then Fernanda called Franco's home and their 10 year old daughter picked up the phone and then gave it to her father and Franco also said he had to discuss it with Sofia and get back to them. After a few minutes, both Mitra and Franco called to let them know that they were on board with the trip to Brazil.

The next day Mitra picked up Fernanda and Sofia and they all went to the gym. On the way, Mitra turned to Sofia and said: "One of our neighbors is going to come to the gym to sign up for one of your aerobics classes. I want you to take good care of her. Her ex-boyfriend use to really give her hell and I suggested that she come to our classes to get some peace.

Sofia: Don't worry! I'll take care of her. What's she like?

Mitra: She's a good person. I'll bring her to you as soon as she shows up.

Fernanda: I have to go to the kid's school for career day. I have to be there for about 2 hours.

Sofia: Good for the kids! Career day and dance at the same time!

Fernanda: That's the fun thing about my job!
At the same time, Ratin and Franco had gone to the customs department and Daniel had gone to the firm on his own when he remembered he had to call his friend about the space trip and ask about the website he had to go one to sign up for the trip. After a few minutes, he got an email in which the date they had to personally go to the space station was announced. The same email was sent to the rest of his friends as well. They were all happy that they had got accepted to go on the space trip and decided to celebrate that night along with their children. Once they were at the restaurant Sofia's daughter, Mary, said: "We want to sit at a different table." The other kids agreed.

Fernanda said: We have to sit at the same table
Fernanda's daughter, Vennessa said: You guys talk about your own stuff and we don't understand a word. You either talk about work or the gym. We three want to talk about our own stuff.
Fernanda: Fine, you guys are all grown up. We can't force you to do anything.
Mitra: The kids are right. There's an empty table next to ours. You guys can sit over there.
The kids were happy they got their way and had their dinner at a separate table.

Sofia turned to Mitra and said: "You guys are lucky you don't have kids. They are either constantly whining or do whatever they want and at the end of the day they are still unhappy.

Mitra: It's okay. Don't forget that you were the same once and use to drive your own parents crazy as well.

Sofia: Yeah, you're right. I sometimes forget how naughty I was.

Mitra raised her glass of wine and said: Cheers to the space trip!

Four days later they all went to NASA based on a previously stated date. Other passengers had already arrived and a number of others were getting in.

Suddenly Fernanda saw the club owner, John, who was there with a number of his customers. He came towards them and said: "I didn't think you guys would be able to afford a trip like this.

Fernanda: You're not the only rich person in town, you know.

John: Well, I guess money solves everything and I can do whatever I want with mine.

Fernanda: Don't count your chicks until they've hatched.

John: I'm gonna be the first person who sets foot onto the shuttle. The more you pay the more you're appreciated.

Fernanda: Hope your dreams come true.

John: All my dreams do come true all I have to do is to make it happen.

Fernanda: I think you also have to be physically fit to go on the space trip.

John: That's not a problem. I can solve everything with money.

Fernanda: Well, then good luck.

This was when someone went behind the podium and said:

Ladies and gentlemen, on behalf of NASA I welcome you all to our site in California. You are all here because you have signed up for this trip and some of you have come from far distances to be here. Today, we have invited those volunteers who live in America. In the first phase of this plan, we have accepted everyone but we will be conducting a series of tests that you have to undertake and pass in order to go to the next selection round. If you fail, it is goodbye and if you pass another final test will be administered in which a fewer number of people will be selected. If the selectees in this phase are too many 40 individuals will be selected based on their scores and 20 of them will be sent to space in the first round and 20 others will be sent in the second round. I wish you all good luck. Now, a number of forms will be distributed among you. I ask that you carefully fill them out.

Franco turned to Ratin and said: I hope we all make it to the next round.

Ratin: Me too.

They all handed in their forms and one by one prepared themselves for the physical test. Ratin was the first among his friends to give the physical test. There were five separate rooms for each test to help move the process along more quickly.

It was 12pm and everyone had finished giving the test and the names were set to be announced after lunch. Two hours later, once everyone had had lunch, someone went behind the podium and said: "Ladies and gentlemen, I know you are all stressed out about the results and I'm sure you all want to be on the space trip but the main condition is your physical and cardiovascular health among other things. So, if you don't hear your name don't be upset. The names I will announce have been rejected in the preliminary tests and will not be able to continue to the next levels."

A number of names were read out and at the end the man behind the podium said: "Those who have been rejected in this phase have been announced. The rest of you please stay here while we say goodbye to the rejected individuals.

Ratin said: None of our names were announced.

They all cheered and Fernanda went towards John and said: "Looks like your money couldn't buy you a trip to space.

John: Don't worry. I'll get in

Fernanda: Well, that's just wishful thinking. You'd better leave now since you were rejected in the first phase.

John left angrily.

The man went back to the podium and said: "Ladies and gentlemen, 74 of you have been accepted in this phase. We will continue testing for three days and 200 individuals will give a test each day. In the end 74 of you will be divided into two groups and you will be asked to come back in five days to enter into the second round of tests."

Ratin turned towards his friends and said: " I'm getting stressed out. There are a lot of volunteers.

Fernanda: I really gave him a piece of my mind. That self-centered bastard! Oh, sorry! Yeah, you're right. Everyone wants to go to space. This is where getting out of the tests is the only way to determine who will be on the shuttle to space. So, we have to give it everything we got. They all got into the car and left. On the way, all Fernanda could talk about was John and how he had not gotten accepted for the trip to space while the others were expressing their concerns regarding the next tests.

Ratin: Guys! What are we doing?!!!! We're supposed to be excited about this trip not disappointed. Let it go! Come what may!

Then he turned to Franco and said: " Why don't we listen to a song to change the mood!"

Franco dropped everybody off and after a couple of days, test day finally arrived and once again they went to NASA. About fifty people had gathered there and the tests began. The NASA manager went behind the podium and said: "Ladies and gentlemen, my name is Steve and I'm happy to welcome you. Two hundred and sixty eight people have been accepted in the first round and 53 individuals have relinquished their request leaving us with 215 volunteers which will be taking the test in the next seven days and today your group will be doing just that. You will be giving the tests in the next seven days. We have done our best to place spouses into the same group so you won't have any transportation troubles so today we are only going to have married couples give the test. "

Mitra looked at Ratin and said: It's a good thing we're in the first group.

Sofia suggested that they make a unity wheel and they all did so and wished each other good luck. Each name was read and one by one they entered the rooms. A four hour recess was announced at noon and after lunch was served Steve said: "Everyone please join me in the adjoining room."

The room was used to administer physical exams for everyone. Once all the phases were complete everyone went home and the results were set to be announced in the next couple of days.

Before leaving Daniel asked Steve: "Can we go on vacation for the holidays?"

Steve: "Of course, my friend. Once the tests are administered we won't have anything else to do for a month given that our volunteers come from all over the world and it would be impossible to gather them all together in a short notice. Go have fun! And happy new year!"

Daniel: Happy new year to you too!

On the way back, Daniel informed his friends that they can still go on their Brazil trip since everything regarding the space trip will be halted for a month.

Sofia: I hope that we all get to go on this space trip.

Mitra: This is what we all pray for.

Franco: We have to wait for the results and then we'll know for sure.

Daniel: Guys, we have to get everything done in the next couple days since Christmas is right around the corner and Brazil awaits us. I'll take care of the tickets.

Mitra: I think we're going to have a blast this year. We'll be getting away from all the snow and the cold for a change.

Fernanda: Yeah, the kids are excited too. They've told all their friend that they're going to take pictures and film the entire thing so they can show it to them once we get back.

They all went home and after a couple of days they were at the airport on their way to Brazil. They were greeted by Fernanda's family at the Brazilian airport and were all invited to their home where they enjoyed fine dining and went to bed early since they were all tired from the long trip.

In the morning, after having had breakfast, Daniel turned to the kids and said: "Pack your things cause we're headed to the woods. And by the way, some of

Fernanda's family members will be joining us.

Franco: What a great idea! The more the merrier! Aren't your family members going to be joining us as well?

Daniel: No, they've gone to Portugal to visit some relatives and will be celebrating New Year's there.

They all headed out after an hour and were on the way for a couple of hours until they reached their destiny. They set up six tents in the jungle and alongside the river and put the two boat they had brought into the water. They also had a number of electrical motors in order to be able to set up a fridge for the food.

Sofia turned to Mitra and said: Guess what would be great for lunch?

Mitra: Are you thinking what I'm thinking?

Sofia: Yes! Fish!

Fernanda went towards them and said: Let's wander around a bit with the boat and see if we can catch any fish.

Mitra: What if we can't catch anything? What should we do for lunch then? Everyone will starve!

Fernanda: Don't worry about it. My family will take care of it! We're just gonna go and have fun fishing! We don't have to catch anything! Fernanda's son, Louise, said: We wanna go fishing too.

Fernanda: Go tell your grandfather and join them. We wanna be alone on the water so we can talk.
Louise said: Oh right I forget. You always wanna be alone.

Fernanda turned to Sofia and said: You see what attitude I have to put up with?
Louise ran away.

Ratin went towards the ladies and said to Mitra: We wanna take a walk in the jungle. Would you guys like to join us?

Mitra: No, thanks honey. We wanna go boat riding.

Ratin: Okay. Have fun then. Take care.

The ladies got into the boat and were only able to catch two fish. They all had fish kebabs for lunch.

At night, Ratin and Mitra gathered everyone together. He stood on a car and said: " Hey everybody, tonight marks Yalda night in the Iranian culture. The longest night of the year, called Yalda night, has been celebrated in our country for centuries. People stay up late and have fruits and nuts and wine and you guys are our guests tonight."

Fernanda translated Ratin's words for his relatives and then added: But we don't have that kind of nuts and fruits that you're talking about. Then he turned to everybody and said: "Guys, Iran has the best nuts! Pistachios, figs, peach pieces, apricots, peanuts, and so many others and most importantly Shiraz wine and the pomegranates that are drank and eaten on Yalda night. The Iranians are one of the oldest civilizations to have grown wine grapes. I remember one year Ratin and Mitra's relative sent them a special fruit called "Chagaleh Badam" and I couldn't get enough of them. I wish we could have some this year too."

Mitra: I'll ask my relatives to send us some.
One of Fernanda's relatives asked: "What is this 'Chagaleh Badam' that you just talked about?"

Ratin explained and Fernanda translated that 'Chagaleh Badam' is grown on almond trees around Shiraz and it is picked from the trees while it's still green and before it's hardened and turns into actual almonds. It has a brittle texture and tastes sour.

Fernanda said: Now that our mouth is dripping, how are we going to celebrate Yalda night?

Ratin: We've taken care of it and we've brought nuts and pomegranates and Shiraz wine with us.

Fernanda: Aahh, you guyssss! Why didn't you say so in the first place?

Mitra: We didn't wanna spoil the surprise!
Then they brought the nuts and the fruits and spent time together eating and laughing. Ratin talked about the past and Shiraz wine was served to all.
Ratin said: I remember when I was a kid. At the end of winter when 'Chagaleh Badam' came to the market and the shop keepers would chant out 'Freshly picked'! Everybody would smell spring in the air and it would remind them that Norooz was right around the corner.

Fernanda's mother said: These nuts are excellent! And the pistachios are delicious!

Ratin: That's why pistachios from Iran are the best in the world.

They all had fun that night and gave the left-over nuts to Fernanda's mother since they had never had such nuts before.

Fernanda joked: What about us?! You gave it all to my family?!!

Ratin: Okay, I'll order a few kilos to be sent just for you. Happy now?

Fernanda: Very.
And they all laughed.

Ratin: Guys we'll have Iranian kebab tomorrow. How's that sound?

Fernanda: Really?!! That would be wonderful!
Then she translated what Ratin had said for her family and they all screamed with joy.

Daniel: Good idea! I love Iranian kebab!

Fernanda's father: You're intimidating us!

Fernanda: Dad, you have to wait till tomorrow.
Then they all went to their tents to rest.
In the morning, Ratin and Mitra starting preparing the ingredients for kebab. Ratin put the meat on the skewers and placed them on the coal and after a few minute a very nice smell filled the air. Everybody

wanted to try a bite and one by one they took the kebabs off of the coal.
They all loved it.

Fernanda's father said: I have eaten a lot of different kinds of meat and
kebab but none of them tasted this delicious.

The others asked Mitra for the recipe.

A few days passed. They spent their time fishing, swimming, water-
skiing, and playing all sorts of games. On the fifth day Fernanda's
phone rang and after having answered it she let out a big scream which
terrified everyone and they all ran towards her. She was jumping up
and down.

Mitra asked: What's going on? Why are you jumping up and down?

Fernanda: I got accepted to go on the space trip!!!
Mitra started jumping up and down with her and showing her
happiness. Everyone laughed at them. After a few minute Fernanda
yelled that she had been accepted to go on the space trip.

Daniel: They only called you?

Fernanda: I'm not sure. Why don't you all check your phones?
They all went to get their phones and Mitra was the first to give out a
scream and say: I got accepted too!!!!!
Ratin had also been accepted but Daniel, Sofia, and Franco didn't say
anything.

Fernanda asked: Why are you guys so quiet?

Daniel and Sofia said that they were not accepted and Franco also said that his attempts had been worthless and he should maybe try again next year.

Ratin: Guys! We all tried and we wanted this to be something we could do together! I guess we shouldn't go either.
Sofia: No, you guys got better grades because of your physical abilities and higher scores. This was a personal test. It has nothing to do with our group. Our emails say we can apply again next time. So, we can give it another shot next year.
Franco and Daniel agreed with Sofia.

Daniel said: We'll go next year.

Fernanda: You mean we three should go? We shouldn't feel guilty about going?

Daniel: Yes, honey. You guys should go with a clear conscience.

Fernanda's mom came up to them. She gave a kiss to Ratin and Mitra and gave Fernanda a hug and wished them good health and success.

Christmas day arrived and they had a big party and went back to America after a couple days of resting in Brazil. They went on NASA's on the appointed day and saw that only 20 people were there. Steve came in and after welcoming them all said: "Ladies and gentlemen, I am very happy to be your host. You are the first group to go on this trip. A beautiful hotel in space is awaiting you all. We have passengers from all over the world; South Africa, France, Canada, Japan, Australia, and many others. Your flight will be in ten months and during this time you will have to physically prepare yourselves for this trip and participate in the training courses. Now, your trainers will provide you with further information in this regard."
At the end of the day, everybody got together and started introducing themselves.

Mitra turned to Ratin and said: Look honey, it's so interesting. A collection of people from all over the world have gathered here, each with their individual nationalities. It's so delightful. When we get up there and see the Earth each person will say I come from a different part of the world. I can't wait for that moment.

Ratin: Me neither.
Then they all went home and were asked to return to NASA in three days. After three months the day they had all been waiting for finally arrived. Everyone had come and a number of news reporters were on the site to broadcast this event. Having said goodbye to their friends

and loved ones, Fernanda, Mitra, and Ratin entered the site and the shuttle was ready for lift off in 3 hours and count-down commenced. They were lifted into the air and gone out of sight. Once they reached the space station and their hotel, everyone was excited. They entered the hotel, everyone had an exhilarating feeling of seeing the earth and being in such a beautiful place. The hotel had two floors and 10 rooms. Each floor had a separate hall and each room had its own cabins from which the guests could enter space. They were going to stay in this hotel for ten days. Seven days went by, each of the guests were able to contact their loved ones from the space shuttle several times. Suddenly, it was announced that meteor had hit the space station and shut down the cameras of both the space station and the hotel. It was also announced that two astronauts had gone to evaluate the situation and repair the cameras. It was said that this is a normal thing and the guests were asked to return to their rooms lock the door and do not exit the hotel in order to remain safe.

Fernanda was in Ratin and Mitra's room and they were dancing and enjoying themselves when they heard the message. They merely locked the door and continued dancing. This was one something unusual happened. An extraordinary creature landed on the moon and looked at Earth and started to quickly fly towards the Earth when he saw a big object and went towards that. It was a broadcasting satellite. He looked at it carefully, not knowing what it really was. He looked around again and noticed the space hotel and quickly approached it. He saw the three astronauts who were repairing the cameras in their special suits. One of them said: "The camera is working for now." This was when another meteor hit the body of the space station and the metal holding one of the astronauts' belts was dislocated and he was dropped into space. He was screaming and asking for help when the alien approached him and held his back. The astronaut was happy that he wasn't falling into space anymore but he was also confused as to who was holding him since he could not see his surroundings. He was moving towards the space station, his friends fascinated at such a scene, could not move a muscle. Finally, he arrived at the station and his friend took his hand and said: "It's a miracle. How could you move in space and make it to the station?"

He replied: I don't really know. But it felt as if someone was pushing me forward.

Right at that moment, one of the astronauts saw a pair of blue eyes behind his friend and said with fear: "Look behind you!"

His friend turned around but there was nothing in sight!

He said to his friend: "Are you going out of your mind? There's nothing there! You're in shock!"

The creature had gone away and was no longer in sight. But the camera that had been repaired had recorded the whole thing. The astronauts went back inside because they couldn't fix the cameras for now and decided they would give it another shot the next day.

The alien took a look around and went towards the space station. It could see the hotel guests but was surprised to see that they looked different than those three astronauts. He snooped around the hotel and was attracted to one of the rooms and carefully stood on its window and saw three people who were doing something unusual and differed from the other guests in the hotel. That was Ratin, Mitra, and Fernanda's room who were dancing. It sat in order to better enjoy the view. When it put its hand on the hotel window, the hands' color changed to match that of the window and his body could be seen and it looked exactly like the window itself. Then he went back and saw that the he had taken the shape of the window. He was surprised, so he meditated and his body went back to its original invisible form. He put his hand back on the window but this time nothing changed. Right at that moment a small object hit the window and the danger alarm went off scaring everyone. The alien went towards the window at the same time that Ratin did and he noticed that the alien had fixed the window and the alarm was no longer going off.

Ratin turned to his friends and said: Hey guys the glass is not broken anymore.

This was when the alarm went off again and the hole in the glass reappeared.

Ratin looked at the window again and surprisingly said: Come look. The window was just fixed and now it's broken again.

His friends saw it and were all astonished. This was when Ratin saw a pair of bright blue eyes that terrified him and made him jump back. He quickly pressed the button that made the metal covers of the window come up and turned off the alarm.

Ratin's friends asked: What's wrong? Why are you terrified?

Ratin: Umm guys, I saw a pair of bright eyes outside!

Fernanda: You're imagining things!

Ratin: No, believe me. I saw someone filling up the gap in the window.

Mitra: Are you sure honey?
This was when someone knocked the door.

Mitra: I'll get it.
She tried to open the door but he couldn't.

Mitra: I think the space object that hit our shuttle has compromised the door.
She then shouted: We're okay! Don't worry about us!
The hotel manager Bill said: We'll do our best to fix the door as soon as possible.
So they all went out of the doorway.

Ratin: You guys don't believe me?

This was when it sounded like something was being hit at the outside door. It seemed like they were trying to open the door.

Ratin: I told you there's something outside.

Mitra: Let's open the door and find out who it is!

Fernanda: But we don't know what's behind that door!

Ratin: Don't worry! We'll figure it out!
He went through the exiting cabin and closed the door behind him. He put on his clothes, wore a mask, and went towards the main exit. He scarily open the door but he didn't see anything so he went back and said: "There was nothing there. "
A few seconds passed so he said to his friends: There's nothing out here. I'm coming back.
He went back into the room, changed, and entered the main room and closed the door behind him. They were all in shock of the sound they had heard behind the door.

Fernanda: Well, it was nothing I guess.
Suddenly they heard an unusual sound that repeated Fernanda's words and said: Well, it was nothing I guess.
They all turned to the sound in extreme shock and fear. They gathered together.

Ratin said: Hello, who are you?

The sound repeated: Hello, who are you?

Mitra said: Guys, there's something here that's mirroring everything we say.

The voice repeated everything Mitra had said.

Ratin said: Show yourself!

The sound repeated: Show yourself!

Ratin pointed to everyone to be quiet. This was when the alien appeared itself and mimed Ratin's gesture of silence. They all froze of fear.

Ratin said scarily: Don't be alarmed! If it was gonna hurt us, it would have done it by now.

The alien moved a step forward and everyone else moved a step back.

It moved further ahead and they moved further back from fear.

It said: Hello, who are you? Show yourself!

Ratin swallowed his fear, went forward and said: Who are you?

And he moved his hand towards the alien and it said: I'm trying to understand your language.

It moved its hand towards Ratin. Ratin took its hand with fear and said: Guys, it looks like glass. Don't be scared. It seems harmless.

The alien touched and observed Ratin's face and body with care. Fernanda and Mitra also went forward and touched it.

Fernanda said: You're so tall! Good for you!

Ratin: I think it's two meters tall, right?

Mitra: Exactly! It looks exactly two meters tall!

A few minutes went by and they each gave their opinion regarding the alien.

Ratin said: Let's go sit next to it and get to know it!

After a couple of hours the alien had learned their language and was able to fluently speak with them. They all became friends with it and asked about its past.

It said: I know nothing about my past and don't remember anything in that regard.

Mitra touched its body and asked: What is your body made of?

Ratin said: It looks like glass but appear to be harder and said to the creature: You look more like a diamond.

The alien said: My body is very tough and hard.

He then petted Ratin's head and said: What are these?

Ratin: We call it 'hair'. Looks like, unlike us, you don't have any. But look at your body! Never in my life have I seen anything like it.

The alien got up and starting walking around.

Ratin said: You have such hard echo-skeleton and yet you move around like a feather.

Suddenly the alien jumped back with fear. They all got worried and went towards it.

The alien said: Someone that looks just like me is standing there.

Ratin: Where?

The alien pointed to the wall.

Ratin took a look, laughed and said: That's a mirror and you are seeing yourself in it. Don't be alarmed.

Then he took the alien by hand and they went towards the mirror.

Ratin stood in front of the mirror and said to the alien: Now, what do you see?

The alien replied: Now, I see you.

Ratin stepped aside: Now, what do you see?

The creature replied: Now, I see myself.

Ratin stepped next to him: Now, what do you see?

The creature replied: Now, I see you and I also see myself.

Ratin said: Go ahead and touch the glass, then you will understand.

The alien went closer and took a closer look at the mirror.

Ratin: Now, do you understand how it works?

The alien replied: Yes, how did you make it?

Ratin: We didn't make it. It was made by other people who live on the planet Earth. By the way would you like us to refer to you as the Diamond Man?

The alien replied: Yes, I like it.

Mitra: And I think it suits you too.

This was when the space hotel manager Bill knocked the door and said: We have informed the space station and we are waiting for them to send someone to fix the door. Can I get you anything in the meantime? We can't use the exit door because of asteroids.

Ratin loudly replied: Don't worry, we're okay.

Then he turned to his friends and said: We can't let them know that the Diamond Man is here.

Fernanda: Why not?

Ratin: Because this is a very rare event that doesn't just happen for everyone. You've probably seen movies about these types of events in which the alien in hidden from others. Don't you think we should keep this to ourselves?

Then he turned to the Diamond Man and said: My friend, if we show you to them they will take you for examinations and we can no longer be with you.

After much debate, they were able to explain the situation to him and attract his attention to the importance of the matter. He agreed with their plan and it was decided that he would make himself invisible once the door was fixed and then he would reappear when others had left the room and with a sign from Ratin.

Mitra said: We were lucky that the cameras were down and couldn't capture the Diamond Man and even luckier that the doors are also closed shut and wouldn't open otherwise everyone would have found out about him and we couldn't help him anymore.

The door was fixed after an hour and Fernanda and Mitra left the room. Ratin stayed and took a look at the broken window with Bill.

Bill said: The important thing is that you closed the metal cover in time. We have to change the glass later. But we have more important matters like the cameras and damaged equipment that have to be attended to at the moment.

While Bill was in the room the Diamond man had made himself invisible and was sitting on a chair waiting for Bill to leave. Bill left after a few minutes and the girls returned and said:

Fortunately, no one has seen the Diamond Man since all the cameras are down. But you have to stay invisible for now and you can reappear at night.

Ratin said: You guys go and join the others so no one suspects anything suspicious is going on.

The girls joined their friends and came back after a while. They closed the door and started talking about different things. A day before their return had arrived and none of the equipment had been fixed.

All three were carefully paying attention to what was going on in the hotel so no one would notice the Diamond Man. They had decided to put him in the shuttle in its invisible form and take him back to Earth. When the time came for them to go back to Earth the Diamond Man placed himself among them so that no one would accidently touch him.

Once they landed on Earth, the Diamond Man flew behind Mitra and Ratin and it was decided that they would take him home since they didn't have any children of their own. After being interviewed and greeted by a mass crowd of people, they finally got into a car and headed home. Mitra and Ratin couldn't stop thinking about the Diamond Man since they didn't want him to get lost so Ratin got out of the car with an excuse to make a call and called out to the

Diamond Man: Where are you my friend?

A voice from behind Rating gently replied: I'm here.

Ratin was startled and said: I didn't think you would be right behind me. We'll be saying goodbye to our friends soon and we'll get home.

They arrived home after 20 minutes and Mitra said: Come on in after us.
All three went in and Ratin closed the door and said: Now, you can reappear. Make yourself at home.

The Diamond Man reappeared and said: You have a beautiful home! So, this is what and Earthly house looks like.

Mitra: Of course, not all Earthly houses look like this. Every country has its own specific architecture. As different as the people living in different countries are, they also have various architecture.

The Diamond Man said: I would like to learn more about Earth.

Ratin said: Come and lay down and watch some TV.

The Diamond Man said: What's a TV?

Ratin: Wait and see.

He turned on the TV and gave the Diamond Man the control and said. Look there are many different channels and each in a different language. The TV can help you understand our world better.

The Diamond Man said: It's really interesting.

Ratin: Yes, it's one of man's greatest inventions.

In Daniel and Fernanda's house, Fernanda told her husband all about the Diamond Man and they also informed Franco and Sofia. It was decided that they would all go and see the Diamond Man the next day.

Ratin told the Diamond Man: You'll meet some new friends in our house tomorrow.

Mitra brought them some juice and sat next to the Diamond Man and said:
Now, I want to know what kind of eating habits you have. Can you drink?

The Diamond Man replied: I don't really know. I've never tried it before.

Mitra handed him a glass of orange juice. He tasted it a bit and said: It's delicious.

Then he drank the whole glass and his body color changed to orange after a while. Mitra and Ratin and even the Diamond Man himself were shocked.

The Diamond Man said: My body color is the exact same color as the juice. His body color went back to normal after a minute.

Mitra said: This is very interesting. Are you craving anything special?

The Diamond man replied: No, I'm not.

Mitra said: We eat all kinds of things. What about you?

The Diamond Man replied: Don't you guys eat the same things that you use to eat when you were in space?

Mitra: No, those were special types of food that we had to eat because we were in space. It's different here on Earth and we can eat all sorts of things.

The Diamond Man: Like what?

Mitra: Iranian Kebab, Shirazi Rice with Cabbage, Vegetable Stew (Aash Sabzi), Vegetable Rice with fish, and many other types of food. I'll explain more latter. What kind of food do you eat?

The Diamond Man said: My food is made of the same material that my body is made of.

Ratin: But you haven't eaten anything so far. You haven't even said you're hungry.

The Diamond Man replied: I rarely eat anything. I only get hungry if my energy is wasted.

Ratin: What about water or liquids?

The Diamond Man: I don't need any liquids. But I liked the juice. I like to try all sorts of drinks that you guys use.

Mitra asked: Where are we supposed to get food for you?

The Diamond Man said: My body becomes sensitive towards rocks and things once it gets hungry and if there's anything to eat around my body would feel it.

Mitra asked: Can you do it now?

The Diamond Man said: Do you want me to gain energy from sources outside my body?

Mitra: Yes.

The Diamond Man said: Ok.

He concentrated and held the juice glass in his hands and said: My body is showing a reaction to this glass cup. Can I eat it?

Mitra: Sure. But how are you going to eat it?

The Diamond Man used the energy in his body to soften the glass and changed it into a doughy texture and slowly began to eat it.

Mitra and Ratin were astonished at such a scene and Mitra started jumping up and down and screaming to release her excitement. The Diamond Man was shocked at her reaction.

Mitra: Sorry, I got carried away. You've never seen such a reaction from me and that's why you are shocked.

The Diamond Man replied: Yes, you were so quiet and calm that such a reaction astonished me.

Ratin: You have to forgive my wife for startling you, she easily gets carried away. You'll get used to it.

The Diamond Man asked: Can I jump up and down like that and scream too?

Ratin: Of course you can.

The Diamond Man started jumping up and down and after a while he jumped higher and higher and his laughs turned into loud screams that broke the entire glasses and lamps in the house and everywhere went dark.

Ratin quickly turned on a light and turned to Mitra and said with surprise: Wow. He's the source of a tremendous amount of energy. We have to be more careful next time.

Mitra turned to the alien and said: I think it would be better if you didn't do that anymore. You scream very loudly and we don't want to attract any more attention than we have to because we could lose you. Whenever you feel like releasing your energy this way all you have to do is tell us and we'll take you out into nature and you can scream all you want.

The Diamond Man said: I don't understand why the lamps and glasses broke?!

Mitra: Interesting. You didn't even know how much energy you have, did you?

The Diamond Man replied: No, I didn't. Because I have never lived among humans before to be able to see how much energy I really have.

Ratin: I'm gonna go get some lamps from the garage. But I have to call the company to come and fix the glasses and windows. Mitra, could you take care of it for me? See if they can send someone right away.

Ratin then went and brought a couple of lamps and asked Mitra: Did you make the call?

Mitra: Yup, they'll be here in less than an hour.

Ratin: I'll take care of the lamps and then I'll clean up the broken glasses. Be careful or you'll hurt yourself.

The Diamond Man said: You don't have to worry about me. I won't get hurt.

Then, they all laughed. Once the lamps were replaced the glasses were cleaned up and the Diamond man suddenly got up and said: Let me help. I want to test my inner energy.

Once he touched the glasses they stuck to his hands.

Then he happily said: I knew I could do it.

Mitra brought the trash bin closer and the Diamond Man through all the glasses into it. Ratin and Mitra were very excited.

Mitra asked: How did you do that? Your body seems to act like a magnet for glasses.

The Diamond Man replied: What's a magnet?

Mitra brought a piece of magnet and explained how it works to the Diamond Man.

The Diamond Man said: Then I'm like a magnet but for glasses. First I attract then repel them. I'm really shocked. I never knew I had such powers. I have to start learning my inner powers.

Mitra: I'm not sure if we got all the glasses or not.

The Diamond Man replied: I'll look around and see if there's anything left.

He drew his hand around the carpets and on the sofa and all over and some glasses stuck to his hands.

He said: It was just a few pieces. Now you can sit on the sofa.

Mitra and Ratin gave the Diamond Man a room in which he could easily rest and be out of any possible guests' sight.

The Diamond Man thanked Ratin and Mitra and said: I'm really grateful to you both for showing me such great kindness.

Mitra said: Make yourself at home. You can do anything you like and eat whatever you want from the fridge.

The Diamond Man said: Thank you. I don't really need anything right now. I'll let you know if I get hungry.

Ratin replied: You can go ahead and rest right here if you're tired.

The Diamond Man: I'm not tired. I'd like to watch TV instead.

Mitra: Great and I can tell you all about different countries and their languages.

The Diamond Man was excited to learn that so many different languages existed and he asked:

-Why do people speak in so many different languages?

Mitra: I can go on and on in order to answer your question. Sometimes, even in a single country more than one language is spoken but in forms of different dialects.

As they were talking about this matter, the doorbell rang.

Ratin said: I'll go downstairs and get the door. They've come to replace the glasses. I'll take care of them.

Mitra and the Diamond Man quickly went into the room.

The Diamond Man asked to see how they were going to change the glasses but Mitra was worried that he might be seen.

The Diamond Man said: Don't worry about it! I'll make myself invisible.

Then they went into the dining room and the Diamond Man carefully watched as the glasses were replaced until they left and the Diamond Man reappeared.

Ratin surprisingly said: Weren't you supposed to be in the room?

Mitra: No, Honey. He was standing here in the dining room the whole time.

The Diamond Man said: They had an interesting job! Let's go and watch some more TV.

They watched TV for two hours and they explained all about the different channels and programs for him until Ratin finally said:

My eyes are too tired. I have to go lie down a bit.

Mitra asked the Diamond Man to go to bed as well but he wasn't tired, so Mitra and Ratin said good night and left him alone while he was watching TV.

When Mitra went to the dining room in the morning the Diamond Man was still watching TV.

Mitra surprisingly asked: Did you wake up early?

The Diamond Man replied: I never went to bed. I have been watching TV this whole time.

Mitra: Really?!!!! Didn't you get tired?

The Diamond Man: No, why should I get tired? I didn't do anything special that would tire me out. All I did was sit here and watch TV.

Mitra laughed and said: You're lucky you don't get tired! Are you hungry?

The Diamond Man replied: No.

Mitra: Our friends are coming over to see you today.

The Diamond Man: Why?

Mitra: Don't be alarmed. You've already met Fernanda on the space trip. She will be coming here with her husband and two of our other friends. They're like family to us. All of us signed up for the space trip but only three of us were lucky enough to go on the trip.

The Diamond Man replied: Ok, I understand. What do I have to do now?

Mitra replied: You don't have to do anything special. This is just a simple get together of friends.

Ratin came into the living room and Mitra explained how the Diamond Man had been up all night.

Ratin: Good for you! You apparently have a lot of power and we shouldn't be surprised at what you can do. By the way, our friends won't be bringing their children tonight.

The Diamond Man asked: Why not?

Ratin replied: Because we don't want the children to know about you since they might get too excited and tell their friends. They're just kids who live in their own little world and don't really understand these kinds of things and consider everything as a kind of game.

The Diamond Man replied: It's interesting how different humans act differently. Even if you are a part of a family there are some things that you cannot reveal to the children.

Mitra: You're quick! Once they get here, I want you to make yourself invisible and then reappear as soon as I call you.

The Diamond Man said: OK.

Ratin was very hungry and wanted to have breakfast but the Diamond Man was fine where he was. Two hours after they had had their breakfast the doorbell rang and Ratin said:

Make yourself invisible and wait by the TV for our signal.

Their friends came in and were very excited and kept asking about the Diamond Man and where he was.

Mitra said: You guys have to wait a little bit.

Sofia: Where is he?

Mitra: Let me put you all at ease and tell you that the Diamond Man is standing is this room and is waiting for my signal to show himself.

Sofia: You mean he's gone invisible right now?

Mitra: He's standing next to the TV.

Sofia: Don't keep us high and dry!

Mitra said: Diamond Man show yourself please.

The Diamond Man reappeared and Mitra and Ratin's friends gasped and screamed with excitement.

The Diamond Man asked: Why are you all screaming?

Sofia replied: Sorry it was a scream out of excitement not fear.

Fernanda told them that they should get up and see him from up close. Sofia, Daniel, and Franco went towards the Diamond Man and touched him.

Mitra said: I'll get some tea while you guys get to know each other.

They spent the whole night getting cozy and talking about the space trip. Once they left the Diamond Man said:

I really enjoyed myself tonight. I'd like for us to have more of such get together.

Ratin assured him that they would have more get together and asked whether he needed anything but the Diamond Man assured him that he was fine and wanted to watch more TV. The next day he asked about computers and the Internet and was curious to learn about it and Ratin promised to teach him everything in the next couple day. After a couple of days, the Diamond Man was easily able to use the Internet and the computer and started web-surfing.

One night the Diamond Man was watching a documentary about Africa which greatly attracted him. Mitra was sitting beside him, explaining about the different types of animals and promised him she would take him to the zoo one day.

The Diamond Man insisted: Let's go now.

Mitra: We can't. It's late and they are closed. Besides, your special clothes are not ready yet. Whenever they're ready we can go anywhere you like.

The Diamond Man said: I'm bored!

Mitra laughed and said to Ratin: did you hear him?

Ratin: Sorry, I wasn't paying attention.

Mitra: He's bored. He's starting to talk and act like us.
They both laughed.

The Diamond man said: Why are you laughing? What did I say?

Mitra: Never mind. We're just talking about how much you have
adapted to our world and our ways.

Ratin: He can help you with the gardening tomorrow since it's a
weekend.
Mitra: Good idea.

The Diamond man said: Thank you. I'm tired of sitting around.
Ratin: I promise to go see the tailor tomorrow and see if we can get the
clothes sooner.
Sunday morning came and after having breakfast Mitra turned to the
Diamond Man and said: Make yourself invisible so no one can see you.

They went to the back yard which was full of beautiful trees and flowers and a pool which was surrounded by glass walls and a beautiful garden.

The Diamond Man said: What's that glass room that's in the water?

Mitra replied: It's a pool. We swim in it. The glass walls protect us from the cold weather outside in the winter.

The Diamond Man asked: What's 'swim'?

Mitra: I'll teach you about swimming once we're done with all the gardening.

The Diamond Man said: I thought only fish swim in the water, like what I saw on TV.

Mitra laughed and said: You're words are so interesting. We swim for fun too. Now, come and see how I water the plants.

She opened the water spray and handed it to the Diamond Man after a while. He enjoyed watering the plants and said:

I can do it on my own. You can go back inside.

Mitra said:

I'll go prepare lunch and be right back.

She returned after ten minutes and saw the Diamond Man cheerfully watering the plants.

Mitra said: I'm glad you enjoy gardening. It's seems as if you've been doing it for a long time. You're a natural!

The Diamond Man asked: Aren't you people patient?

Mitra: We are. But not everyone is like us. Some people are always in a rush. Human beings are different.

Then she said: I think that's enough for today. I'll close the faucet and we'll hit the pool.

The Diamond Man said: I wasn't to learn more about swimming.

Mitra said: Don't worry about it, you're a fast learner.
Then she took off her clothes and went into the pool.

The Diamond Man asked: Why did you take off your clothes?

Mitra replied: We have to wear special swim-ware when we go swimming or else swimming in this season would be very difficult.
The Diamond Man asked: Why? Didn't you say the glass walls are to protect you from the cold?

Mitra: We warm up the water as well so that our body can fight against the cold. Otherwise, we might die from the cold.

The Diamond Man said: Now, I understand. It's interesting. Why is half of your body out of the water?

Mitra replied: Because the depth of the water here is only 1 meters and it increases on the other end of the pool. You can slowly come into the pool, but make yourself visible again so I can teach you how to swim.

The Diamond Man made himself visible and entered the pool, slowly walking he said: It feels so nice. I like the water.

Mitra took his hand and they slowly went towards the deeper end of the pool and explained how he could make himself weightless to stay on the water. He was a fast learner.

Mitra: You're a natural. Good job! Now I want to teach you swimming, doggy style!

The Diamond Man: Why do you call it doggy style?

Mitra: Because it's based on how animals swim and since dogs are common pets kept in human homes we call this type of swimming 'doggy style'.

Then Mitra swam in a doggy style in front of him and he tried it as well. For a minute he went under water and came up with fear. Mitra quickly grabbed him and dragged him upwards and said:

Don't be scared! This always happens the first time around.

The Diamond man said:

I was so scared for a minute because I couldn't keep myself afloat.

Mitra asked: Couldn't you breathe under water? Or are you just like us when it comes to us breathing under water?

The Diamond Man replied:

I don't really know.

Mitra suggested:

Why don't you make yourself light so that you can go deep into the water and if you feel like you can't breathe I'll come and drag you back up.

The Diamond Man replied:

Sounds like a plan. I want to see how strong my body is.

They stayed under water for about a minute when Mitra could no longer hold her breath and gestured to the Diamond Man that she was going back up. They repeated this process several times until they realized that he could easily breathe even under water.

Mitra said: I wish I could hold my breath under water as long as you can.

The Diamond Man replied: I'm glad I could learn more about another one of my capabilities. I just don't understand why I was afraid of going deep into the water at first.

Mitra said: It may be because you didn't really know your boundaries. Now practice as much as you like.

After a couple minutes of practicing he had completely mastered the art of swimming and keeping his breath under water.

Mitra said: Good job! You did it!

Then she went out of the pool and sat there watching the Diamond Man swim.

Ratin came in and said: Great! You've learned how to swim!

The Diamond Man replied:

Yes, Mitra helped me learn. I love it!

Suddenly, he went under water and quickly swam. Ratin and Mitra were surprised how quickly and easily he could swim under water.

Ratin said: He's so fast!! How can he swim so fast under water?

Mitra replied: He doesn't need as much oxygen as we do and he can easily swim under water without having to take breaths.

Ratin said: Then he's really lucky to have such great strength. I wish we could be like him.

The Diamond Man came out of the water and said:
Guys, I love the water! I think I'm gonna do some more swimming. You guys can go back inside. I'll join you whenever I get worn out from all the swimming.
Before leaving him in the pool, they asked him to make himself invisible again so others wouldn't see him. At noon, Ratin, who had been spending time in the garden, went back home but the Diamond Man was not back yet. When he asked about him, Mitra said that he was still swimming.

Ratin said: He's just like kids who never get sick of swimming. Of course, I don't really think that he ever gets exhausted.

Mitra replied: You're right. He doesn't even get tired of watching too much TV. By the way. Did you hear from the tailor?

Ratin replied: I have his clothes right here. I'll go give them to him.

He went to the pool but there were no traces of the Diamond Man. No wrinkles in the water and no traces of movement. He softly called out to the Diamond Man and saw signs of movement in the water.

Ratin said: You were so quiet.

The Diamond Man replied:

I was swimming at the bottom of the pool.

Ratin said: But I couldn't see any traces of you in the water.

The Diamond Man replied:

I've mastered the art of swimming. Now, I can swim without making the water move.

Ratin said: That's great! You're amazing! Let's go back inside. Your new clothes are here!

The Diamond Man got excited and quickly got out of the pool. Mitra dried him up with a towel. Then he put on the suit that had been sewn for him along with a gray mask and soft gloves. The Diamond Man asked:

Why do I have to wear a mask and gloves?

Ratin: So that you're not seen. We want to go out and spend some time amongst other people so we have to very cautious.

Then he said:

Come and see how you look!

The Diamond Man took a long and nice look at himself and said:

I can barely recognize myself now that I'm dressed like this.

Ratin said: We have ordered a series of clothes for you but the tailor had only prepared this one. It'll have to do for now and the rest will be ready in a couple of days.

Mitra asked: This suit is too formal. I think it would be better if we only took him out at night. I'm wondering how we can stop people from touching him or what we should say if they ask why he's wearing a mask.

Ratin: I've thought about it. I think we should tell people that he is a burn victim and the mask and gloves are used to cover his burns.

Mitra: Good thinking! But since we've got used to him we forgot to focus on some details in his clothing.

Ratin asked: What do you mean?

Mitra: Well, we were careful in covering his face and the front part of his body but we forgot to cover him from behind the head.

Ratin: Oh, no! You're right! What are we supposed to do about that?

Mitra:All we have to do is get some wigs for him. But this means we can't go out today. Sorry Diamond Man!

The Diamond Man said:
That's too bad. I was really looking forward to going out today.

Mitra said: Don't worry. I'll go and buy you some wigs tomorrow so you can easily go out whenever you want. I'll also get you some outdoor clothes that are more comfortable and less formal so that you don't attract too much attention and can easily go out.

Ratin agreed and the Diamond Man watched TV. The next day Mitra and Ratin went to buy some wigs for the Diamond Man and he went for a swim.
While the Diamond Man was swimming in the pool one of the neighbors, David, saw a movement in the pool from the rooftop. He thought one of the neighbors was swimming in the pool and wanted to say hi. The Diamond Man noticed that he was being watch and quickly stopped swimming. David noticed the waves in the pool but was surprised to see no one in it and thought to himself how quickly that person had gone out of the pool that it had escaped his notice. He ignored it and went on with his chores and the Diamond Man, who thought that David could no longer see him, continued to swim. The same thing happened a few minutes later and this time the water tide was really high. David thought maybe they had forgotten to turn off the

water pump. He went to the attic to put back some tools when he noticed a very bad smell. He thought it might be a dead rat so he opened the window to let in some fresh air. When he did so, he saw the stormy pool and said to himself: 'It seems as if there's someone swimming in the pool.' He opened and closed his eyes a couple of times and thought to himself 'how is it possible that no one is swimming in the pool and yet there is so much movement in the water?'. He started cleaning up the attic and found the source of the bad smell, which was a dead rat, threw it into a garbage bag and kept looking out the window at the pool. He wondered: 'A water pump could not cause such wrinkles in the water and there must be something else there, but what exactly'. Then, the Diamond Man came out of the water. The neighbor noticed some water being splashed out of the pool. The Diamond Man lied down next to the pool to dry himself up. David was completely confused and after staring at the pool for 10 minutes he was about to close the window when the Diamond Man put his foot into the pool and started to move it. David thought to himself: 'This can't be caused by a pump! A pump doesn't just turn on and off like that! Why is water moving around the pool like that? Maybe their pool is different! I can't understand what's going on! Maybe this is all in my head and the hallucinations caused by the war are back again! I have to call my doctor!'. Then he went and called his doctor and made an appointment. At noon, Ratin and Mitra returned him with a bunch of clothes and wigs.

The Diamond Man happily tried on the different clothes and wigs and said:

I love them all! When can we go out?

Mitra said: We can go out tonight!
The Diamond Man asked: Why tonight? Can't we go out right now?

Ratin said: Let's go out tonight so we can make sure that nothing goes wrong. It's less crowded at night so we will be attracting less attention. At night, they were all excited to go out.

Ratin asked Mitra to quickly send the Diamond Man out once he had turned on the car so that the neighbors wouldn't notice him. Everything went according to the plan. Ratin drove slowly so the Diamond Man could enjoy the view of the city and ask whatever he wanted. After an hour of driving they decided to have dinner.

Mitra said:We should go somewhere that is not too crowded so we're not noticed.
Twenty minutes later they arrived at the restaurant. Everyone looked at them with amazement. Mitra took the Diamond Man by hand and they entered the restaurant and sat in one corner. When the waiter came to hand them the menu he turned to the Diamond Man and said:
What a beautiful mask! It reminds me of the Masquerade!

Mitra replied:

Yes, our friend is a burn victim. That's why he has the mask.

The waiter replied:

I'm so sorry. I'll bring your order as soon as possible.

Once the waiter was out of sight

Mitra said: It's a good thing we came up with the burn excuse or else he never would've left us alone.

Ratin and the Diamond Man changed their spots so that the latter could sit with his back to the entry in order to attract less attention.

The waiter brought their three pizzas, salad, and drinks, apologized again and left.

The Diamond Man asked:What should I do now? It's not like I can eat anything.

Mitra replied:

You just sit and relax. We'll have some of your food so no one would notice that you didn't touch it in order to cause less suspicion when the waiter comes back to bring us our check and clean up.

After paying for dinner and leaving the restaurant

Ratin asked:Should we go back home? I think we've wandered around enough for one night.

Mitra left the decision with the Diamond Man and he said:

Let's go home. I thought since you guys were so close and comfortable with me others would be the same but now that we came out I noticed how different I really am. Let's go home.

Mitra said: Don't be upset. Being different has an upside. This way you can easily go among people and no one would notice how different you are.

The Diamond Man replied:

But, they all looked at me so differently. Didn't you notice the look on the waiter's reaction?

Mitra said: This reaction is completely normal. It's because you're wearing a masquerade mask when there's no masquerade to go to. Many burnt patients wear masks to hide their scars. They stare at you because you're so tall, good looking, and you have a beautiful mask on. All the women were staring at you. Now, I think we should go to the amusement park. What do you think? Let's go have some fun! What do you say?

The Diamond Man said: I want to experience everything. Let's go. Then, they went to the amusement park. All the families and the children would stare at the Diamond Man. They were standing in line for a ride when the family behind them who had two kids noticed the Diamond Man and one of the kids asked his mother: 'Mom, why is that man dressed like that?'

Mitra turned to them and said: He's been burnt so he has to wear this mask to cover his scars.
The child's mother apologized but Mitra said it's ok.
Then the Diamond Man asked the boy if he would like to touch the mask and when the child did so he smiled and then they left for the rides.

The Diamond Man asked: What kind of place is an amusement park?

Mitra answered: It's a place full of excitement and fun and most people scream when they go on the rides. But you have to be careful not to scream or else you know what will happen, right?

They got in line for the ferry wheel and a little girl started nagging her father to buy her a mask like the one the Diamond Man was wearing. Her father turned to the Diamond Man and said:

I'm sorry did you get your mask from around here?

The Diamond Man replied that he had not bought it from the amusement park. Mitra immediately mitigated and said to the father:

No, we bought it from somewhere else.

The little girl's father asked if he could buy the mask from them and when he heard that the mask was used to cover burn marks he apologized and asked for the store's address. Mitra told him that they had ordered it online and that family thanked them and left. They got on the ferry wheel and the Diamond Man was very much enjoying himself and he said:

Human beings have such interesting hobbies! I like your way of life.

Then they went bowling and the Diamond Man kept getting straight strikes and won a bunch of prizes. When he stepped aside to let Mitra and Ratin play, a bunch and kids came up to him and started making fun of him. Ratin noticed what was going on and made the kids go away.

The Diamond Man asked: Why were they behaving like that?

Ratin replied: Not all humans are good people. Some like to hurt others. But please don't use your inner powers against them.

Mitra suggested that they call it a day and go home. When they were on their way back, Franco called and said that they would be dropping by to discuss something with them. Ratin told them that they would get home in half an hour and by the time they got home Franco and Sofia arrived as well.

Ratin asked what was going on that they couldn't talk about over the phone.
Franco took a seat and said:

We saw something unusual on TV tonight. NASA has captured an image from one of the cameras that had been repaired while we were in our rooms of the moment the astronauts were saved. And this footage shows a pair of blue eyes as well.

Ratin asked: Really? You mean it shows the Diamond Man?
Franco replied:

Yes, but since he was invisible at the time the only thing that is seen for a few seconds are his two blue eyes and then they disappear as well.

Once they had given them the news, Franco and Sofia went home. At the same time, Mitra and Ratin's neighbor, David, had also heard the news about the space station and a pair of blue eyes. He was thinking whether he was really hallucinating or not. The next day, he went to see his doctor and since all the examinations were normal his doctor suggested that his hallucinations may be the result of damage caused by explosions during the war. He told David to ignore the hallucinations and he would feel better after a while. David went home but he couldn't stop thinking about what he had heard on the news as well as what he had seen in the pool. He went back to the attic and took another look at the pool but all was calm.

Two days later, the Diamond man went out to water the plants but all David saw was a water hose that was dangling up in the air. He go startled and thought to himself: 'My God, I must be hallucinating again!' He sat in the attic for a while and then took another look at Ratin's garden and noticed the water hose moving and watering the plants on its own. Then he noticed that it fell down and the water was shut off and the same thing happened with that he had seen a couple days ago. At that moment, Mitra came out and called the Diamond Man to go inside and watch TV. Luckily, at that moment David was calling his doctor and did not see Mitra.

At home, after the Diamond Man was finished watching the nature channel he reminded Mitra that they had promised to take him to the zoo. At the same time David looked out the window and noticed that nothing was going on in the pool and he decided that he had gone mad and he made an appointment with his doctor again in the afternoon.

Ratin and Mitra decided to take the Diamond Man to the zoo the next day. When the TV program about animals ended, Ratin switched to the news. The anchor announced that a dangerous child molester and kidnapper had escaped prison by killing two prison guards and taking their weapons. His picture was all over the news and the police spokesman asked all citizens to watch their locks since it was said that the criminal is an expert at picking locks and stealing children from their own homes.

When the Diamond Man heard this he said:
What a horrible human being!

Ratin replied: Yes, he's easily escaped prison and it's so scary to think that he can open any lock.

Mitra suggested: I think people should place some heavy objects behind their doors so he can't break in.

Ratin said: That's a good idea. They should announce it on the news.

The Diamond Man said: Do you think we should put something behind the door too?

Mitra and Ratin laughed.

The Diamond Man asked: Why are you laughing?

Mitra said: Because we don't have any kids. Anyhow, a criminal should be crazy to come to this house!

The Diamond Man asked: Why's that?

Mitra replied: Because we have you to take care of us!
They all laughed.

In the afternoon, David went to see his doctor and was given a couple of tranquilizers to calm him. He was also asked to return in a couple of days for a full CT scan.

The next day, the Diamond Man got up early in the morning and started to watch TV, waiting for Mitra and Ratin to wake up. Once, Ratin woke up the Diamond Man asked to go to the zoo only to realize that he had forgotten to put on his special clothes. They had their breakfast and headed to the zoo. The

Diamond Man said: I'm so glad we're finally going to the zoo. I've seen many animals on TV. It would be great to see them up close. After half an hour of driving, they arrived at the zoo. They got out of the car, bought their tickets and went in. That day was also a school had brought their student for a field trip to the zoo.

The Diamond Man said: I like the children. They're not as serious as grown-ups.

They started from the monkey cages. The zoo was filled with the screams of children and everyone was unaware of the fact that the wanted criminal had hidden himself amongst the crowd and was planning on attacking the children. He had hidden himself in a corner, pretending to watch the birds, while in reality he had the children under surveillance and was plotting to cause a disturbance in the crowd so he could get close to them. He slowly approached the lion cages, unlocked them, and waited for the children to come close.

Then he left the doors to the lions' cages wide open and yelled:

Run away! The lions are loose!

Everyone started screaming and running around. One of the lions noticed the open door and came out of the cage and started running towards the children.

Ratin and the Diamond Man, who were standing a bit further away from the lions' cages, noticed the screams and asked what was going on. Someone told them what had happened and quickly ran away. The Diamond Man quickly ran towards the lions. Three of the lions each attacked him from different sides and he fought all of them off. He slammed two of lions to the walls and made them unconscious. He was still fighting the third one and at this point all of his clothes had been torn up and his diamond body could easily be seen. The zookeepers arrived and the Diamond Man hit the lion on the head with a punch and the lion fell down. The zoo keepers shot all the lions with needles that made them unconscious. Suddenly, the Diamond Man grew afraid of being identified and took off everything and made himself invisible.

Ratin was startled as well and thought to himself: Good job making himself invisible!

Everyone was in shock. The Diamond Man went towards Ratin and Mitra and asked them to take him home. They were headed towards the car when they heard a scream. They turned back and learned that the wanted criminal had taken one of the kids hostage and the zoo guards had followed him and were pointing guns at him. The Diamond Man approached him from behind, hit him on the head, and made him collapse. Then he threw the gun towards the guards and the criminal was easily arrested and the child set free. The police arrived and took the man away. Investigation into the affair started immediately and the security cameras at the zoo were checked. Everyone was shocked and they started talking about an unusual creature who had disappeared and nothing remained of him but a pair of gloves, a mask, and some clothes.

Mitra said: Let's go before they suspect anything.

They immediately left for the house. The guards who had seen everything with their own eyes gave their reports to the police chief commander as well as the zoo officials. The recorded films from the security cameras were viewed and everyone looked at each other with amazement asking who or what this creature was that was able to fight off a bunch of lions with getting a single scar, appeared to be like glass, and made himself invisible and ran away; questions with no answers in sight.

Once Mitra and Ratin got home,

Mitra said: What an unusual day! If it weren't for the Diamond Man those lions would have ripped all those kids apart! What a disaster it would have been! Now, everyone wants to know who he is and his clothes mask and gloves were left behind!

Ratin replied: No need to worry! No one will be able to find him! Oh wait, what if they identify us through the camera?!!!!

After a long discussion they found a solution. The police had discovered the fact that the Diamond Man had been in Mitra and Ratin's car and they were able to find their address based on their license plate. Several police cars as well as the chief police himself set off towards Ratin and Mitra's house. When Ratin saw them from the upstairs window he asked the Diamond Man to make himself invisible so he wouldn't be seen. The Diamond Man said he would go to the garden and he left the house.

Ratin opened the door on the cops and they searched the entire place but there was no trace of the Diamond Man.

The police chief asked Ratin and Mitra: Where is that creature? The one you brought to the zoo!

Ratin replied: What are you talking about?

The police chief said: Don't mock me young man! The zoo camera show you entering the zoo with that creature.

Mitra replied: I'm sorry. We saw a giant man hitchhiking on the road towards the zoo. We gave him a lift. He wanted to go to the zoo.
The police chief asked:

Didn't you notice anything suspicious about him? Didn't you ask why he was wearing a mask?

Mitra replied: We did, actually. But he said that his entire body had been injured in a fire and that's why he's wearing a mask. How should we have known that he's an unusual creature?!!!?!!! We only talked to him for a few minute. Then with what happened at the zoo we realized who he was.

Given that the police had no solid evidence to further investigate them, they left the premises. But the chief police asked them to stay in town. When the TV broadcasted the news about the zoo that night, David was shocked to hear it and did not understand what was going on. He thought to himself: 'This is no longer a hallucination! It's on TV for God's sake!' Then he called one of his friends who was a secret agent and told him everything. His friend said he would drop by the next day to talk. Ratin also called his friends and told them everything and asked them to be more cautious.

In the morning, Alec, who was an intelligent secret agent police officer, went to David's home and asked:

What's going on? Why did you want me to come down here?

David replied: I've noticed something unusual in my neighbor's house lately. At first I thought I might be hallucinating so I just ignored it and went to see my doctor. He thought it may be because of the war injuries and I thought the same until I heard about what had happened at the zoo.

Alec asked: What does what happened at the zoo yesterday have anything to do with what you're talking about?

David replied: I have a feeling that same creature is living in the next door house.

Alec said: Seriously?!!!

David replied: Yes. He swims in the pool and waters the plants.

Alec: Are you sure you're not hallucinating?

David: Yes, I'm sure. I may have had my doubts before but since I learned of yesterday's incident and saw the police pour into their house I am now certain that something is going on there, even though the police couldn't prove anything.

Alec: I don't know! I'm too confused! What are you after exactly?

David answered: Help me identify that creature!

Alec answered: How?

David suggested: We'll place cameras in different places to catch him red-handed.

Alec said: I just hope you're right about this and it isn't another hallucination.

David said: We've known each other for a while. You know me. You know I wouldn't be fixating on this if I wasn't sure there's something going on.

Alec said: Fine. I'll trust your instincts. But we have to keep a low key. This has become a big deal now. I'll get everything ready by tomorrow.

The next night Alec came with everything that was need to set up the surveillance. They set up the camera late at night so no one would notice. They stared at the monitor for hours until Alec got too tired and decided to go home and return the next day.

The next morning David sat behind the monitors but there was still nothing going on. He went to make some coffee and when he went back he noticed that unusual movement in the pool. He quickly called Alec and he got there in fifteen minutes. The camera and sound recorders recorded everything. Alec came in and stared at the monitors with surprise. The Diamond Man swam for about two hours and then dried himself with a towel that was next to the pool, put it back and went home.

Alec said:
What on earth was that?!!!! You were right! That creature is here! But why is it living with them? How does it know them? I have to go and ask some questions about these neighbors of yours.
He came back after a couple of minutes and said:

How well do you know your neighbors?

David replied: Not that well. We're on saying hello when we bump into each other basis. They live behind my apartment and sometimes bring me fruit from their garden. So, I don't know them that well.

Alec said: The interesting thing about them is that they just got back from that space trip. So, I told my boss about this and I'm thinking I have to take all the films related to what happened at the zoo and the space station and the two blue eyes that saved the astronauts to make some further investigations.

Alec copied everything onto his flash drive and left. Once he showed the videos to his boss, his boss said:
We have to instate a secret operative tem around their house tonight.

The cops installed a recorder and infrared cameras in the location and Alec was appointed as head of operations. They also installed some monitors and other types of equipment in David's house. They recorded everything that was going on in Ratin's house for two days and they also listened to all their conversations and phone calls and after gathering enough evidence, the authorities decided to issue a warrant for their arrest.

In the afternoon, all the forces, which had infrared cameras on their masks, went to Ratin's house. Ratin asked the Diamond Man to make himself invisible and then opened the door. Alec and the chief commander showed Ratin their search warrant and started searching the entire house but found no trace of the Diamond Man.

Alec said to Ratin: You're hiding something in this house.

Ratin replied: I don't know what you're talking about.

Alec said: Actually, you do! You better cooperate or else you'll get in a lot of trouble.

Then he ordered his forces to show them all the recorded films and audio files. The film that had been recorded showed the Diamond Man swimming.

Alec said: And these are the last words you just said a few minutes ago. Then he played Ratin's voice which was telling the Diamond Man to make himself invisible. Ratin had nothing to say.

Alec continued: Now what do you have to say for yourself? We have kept you under surveillance for a couple of days and we've recorded everything you've said.

Mitra replied: But he's harmless and you have no right to arrest him.

Alec said: Oh, really?! But I 'can' arrest the two of you and make sure you spend a long time behind bars.

Ratin replied: Then do it. Because we won't hand him over.

Alec ordered for the officers to put the both of them under custody and handcuff them. They were about to take them down to the police station when they heard a voice say:

Wait, I'm here.

The Diamond Man was standing next to the TV when he reappeared and all the officers pointed their guns at him and Alec said:

Stand down and surrender!

The Diamond Man said: There's no need for any of this! I will surrender to save my friends

Ratin said: You don't have to do that.

The Diamond Man replied: You're my only friends and I'm no part of your family. That's what you said yourselves, isn't it?

Ratin: Yes, it is. We're a family.

Alec said: Put him under arrest and take him away.

The Diamond Man said: You can't make me go with you but I will and there's no need for handcuffs. All I ask is that you remove my friends' handcuffs as well.

Ratin said: He's right. You better listen to him.

Alec paused for a minute, then said: Fine. Take off their handcuffs.

One of the officers said: But sir, they're dangerous.

Alec replied: Do as I say!!!!!

They all got into the police cars and headed towards the National Security office where some NASA officials as well some government officials were gathered. Each individual was interrogated separately and since their confessions were synchronized, the officials had no choice but to accept the fact that they were telling the truth. So, they put them into the same room and everyone else heard whatever was said from behind the glass wall.

The inspector asked: Why did you bring this creature back to Earth with you?

Ratin replied: He was headed towards Earth anyway, he merely decided to accompany us back to Earth.

The inspector continued:

What were you planning on doing with him exactly? What was your plan?

Ratin interrupted him:

Hang on a second. If you're trying to make a threat to national security out of this, just stop! You know better than we do that no one has been harmed so far and we never planned anything that would threaten national security. You've been tapping all of our conversations so you should know if we have been plotting an evil plan. Besides, the Diamond Man has shown nothing but good manners towards us.
The inspector asked:

How can we be sure that he won't hurt anyone?

Ratin replied: Think about it. Who saved the astronauts?

The inspector replied: He did.

Ratin said: Exactly! And he didn't even know us then so we couldn't have asked him to do that. He could have just as easily hurt other rather than saving them. He also fought off those loose lions at the zoo and helped you arrest that murderer, didn't he? He's a gentle creature.

The inspector said: I have to agree with you but I don't make the decisions around here.

Mr. Jason, the head of National Security, entered the room and said: I've heard everything.

Ratin said: Let us go. You know where we live and you can keep an eye on us as long as you want.
Mr. Jason consulted with his tem and said:

We have to do some research on this Diamond Man so he has to stay.

The Diamond Man said: I don't have to do anything if I don't want to and you can't make me either. I'll only cooperate if my friends as me to do so as a favor.

Ratin said: Let us take him home and we'll bring him to you whenever you want.

The Diamond Man said: I agree with Ratin. I'll stay if they stay.

Mr. Jason said: That's fine. You can go but we expect you back here first thing tomorrow morning at 8. You know you're under surveillance so you better not do anything fishy.

Ratin replied: You don't have to worry about us. We'll be here in the morning.

They went home, escorted by the security forces, had dinner, watched TV, and went to bed.
In the morning, the Diamond Man made himself invisible and as they were leaving the premises one of the security forces stopped them and asked where the Diamond Man was.

Ratin replied: We're headed towards the research center and the Diamond Man is with us.

At that moment, the Diamond Man grabbed the police officers arm and said hello. The officer was shocked and replied with a hello.

The Diamond Man said: Can you feel me now?

The police officer said: Yeah, I got it. I have to take you to the headquarters. Please get in the car.

They got to the headquarters with a bunch of other cars escorting them. Once they arrived, they made the Diamond Man lay down on a bed and a bunch of doctors and researchers did some research on him. Their research lasted for two weeks. Everyone at the research center had befriended the Diamond Man and he felt comfortable among them.

That afternoon, Ratin and Mitra took the Diamond Man home.

Ratin said: Tonight's the big game!

Mitra said: We're too tired otherwise we would have gone to the stadium and watched the game up close.

Ratin: Why don't we call our friends and ask them to come over so we can watch the game together?

Mitra said: Good idea.

They all got together and Mitra and Ratin's house to watch the hokey game between New York Rangers and Los Angeles Kings which was hosted in L.A. an estimated audience of 10,000 were seated in the stadium. A few minutes after the game had started a terrorist group attacked the stadium and killed a bunch of security guards. They shut down the doors to the stadium and took everyone hostage. There were a lot of them and they all had weapons and were wearing masks that would protect them against any chemical gases that they were going to use.

A bunch of them were in charge of guarding the doors and the rest were stationed in different positions throughout the stadium. The head of the group and a bunch of others attacked the filming and broadcasting section of the stadium and took control of it by firing some shots. Then, he announced that all the doors had been rigged with chemical bombs and his forces had taken control of the entire stadium. Then he warned everyone to be quiet and calm and not make any wrong moves. Everyone was startled and many of the people there started crying and screaming. Once again it was announced that if anyone made any noise, they would be killed. The entire stadium fell to silence. The game was being broadcasted live so the entire city was witnessing every event and everyone was startled.

Ratin said: What a disaster!

The terrorists announced that the players should stay in the field and not move. Suddenly, one of the people in the audience who was carrying a gun killed one of the terrorists. The others chased him to the bathroom and since he was out of bullets they killed him and threw his body onto the field. Everyone was scared and the entire police force had surrounded the stadium and had announced a state of emergency. The head of the terrorist group appeared in front of the cameras and said:

We have chemical bombs installed throughout the entire stadium and if our demands are not met we will explode the entire stadium. Our demands are: 1. Free twenty of my group members who have been arrested. 2. One million dollars cash and 3. A Boeing 747. You don't have much time so you can call the stadium phone and will do the negotiations.

The entire country was witnessing the events going on. And news got to the White House. The President ordered to have all their requests granted. The police commander, Jim, called the stadium and talked with the head of the terrorist group and got the list of names of the 20 prisoners he wanted to be freed and realized how grave the situation really was and informed the President.

The President said: We can't allow a human catastrophe like this to take place. They've endangered so many people. I've already signed the release for those prisoners and the money will be ready soon. The air force is also on standby and the Boeing will be ready soon. Just make sure they take the deal without causing any trouble.

Jim said: Yes, sir! No need to worry! We'll do our best! We are evacuating the city.

The President replied: Good work! Chemical bombs are no joke! You can go and take care of everything!

Jim replied: Yes sir! I'll be in touch.
On the other hand, the Secretary of Defense entered the President's office and said:
Sir, the city is being evacuated. The airport has been cleared out. All flights have been cancelled and all forces are on standby.

The President said: We're stuck in a dangerous situation.

The Secretary of Defense replied: It's like a warzone.

The terrorists had used a device in the stadium to deactivate all cell phones and also the internet so no one can contact anyone outside of the stadium. They've also brought a bunch of bomb rigged cars in the parking and the entire stadium has been rigged with bombs. There were so many bombs that no one dared attack the stadium. Jim talked with the terrorist head but wasn't able to convince him to free the hostages. Jim asked him to at least say his name. The

terrorist said: You can call me Alex. You're running out of time. You only have 10 minutes to prepare the money I asked for.
Please, at least release some of the hostages.

Alex replied: You're running out of time. You only have ten minutes to get me my money. You better not waste it.

Jim said: You never gave us a timeframe for 10 minutes of it to be remaining.

Alex replied: Don't argue with me. I make the decisions and I say that you now have only 3 minutes left.

Jim argued:That's not enough time to prepare the money. We're working on it.
Alex replied:
You're three minutes is already up!

Jim begged: Please don't hurt anyone. We'll get you your money as fast as possible. You can count on it.

Alex merely said:Your time is up.
And he hung up. Jim ran to call the President's office and told them everything. Everyone was worried about what Alex was planning to do. The terrorists pulled 10 random people out of the hostages and shot them to death. Everyone was scared to death.

Mitra screamed and said: Guys! We have to do something! They're killing innocent people.

At the same time Jim called the stadium and asked:Why did you do that? !!!!!

Alex said:I had warned you that your time is up! If you don't get me my money in one hour 10 more will be killed! Prepare the money and then call me!

He hung up! Then the terrorists moved the bodies to a parking nearby and asked the pretend victims to open their eyes. No one had been actually killed. Those 10 people were merely terrorists themselves who had put on a show in order to cause fear and chaos. They took some chemical masks from the car and guns and went back inside. The money Alex had asked for was in his account in 20 minutes. Once Jim informed him of this decision there was a celebration among the terrorists which scared the people there.

Then Jim called the President and let him know that the prisoners were ready to be sent off to the stadium.

The President said:

I hope everything goes smoothly.

Jim replied: Sir, these people are truly terrifying. There's no way we can get to them with negotiating. We have no choice but to give them whatever they demand. They won't even consider releasing some of the hostages.

The President said: What are we to do with such lunatics and their bombs?!
Jim replied: Sir, we'll do our best to draw them out of the stadium and into the plane where we have better choice of succeeding.

The President ordered: Then get them out of that stadium.
On the other side of town, Ratin's house was full of fear and chaos. The

Diamond Man said: Let me go help the people.

Daniel replied: A chemical bomb is no joke! They might set it off and all those people will be killed! Then the entire city will be in danger and we would have to evacuate it!
At the same time, the car containing the prisoners arrived at the stadium and Jim informed Alex so he would open the door and let them in. Everyone was worried about what would happen next. The entire city was terrified and everyone was evacuating it.

Fernanda said: We have to evacuate the city! Don't you think so?!

Ratin replied:I'm thinking of helping the people. Why don't we let the Diamond Man do something!

Sofia asked:Like what?

Ratin continued:Well, he can make himself invisible and then he can do all sorts of things. He may be able to help the cops once the terrorists move to the plane.

Sofia suddenly screamed: OH MY GOD!!!!! We forgot all about our kids!!!!!!!!

Fernanda, Daniel, Sofia, and Franco immediately left to pick up their kids and head out of the city.

Ratin called Alec and told him how they could help. He was told to wait for a call back. Once the President was informed a meeting was held and it was decided that they could use the Diamond Man's special powers in this regard. Alec informed Ratin of the decision and asked him to meet him at the stadium. On the way, Mitra informed their friends of how the Diamond Man was going to help the police. Her friends informed her that they were evacuating the city, so that Mitra and Ratin no longer had to worry about them.

On the other hand, Jim called Alex and asked:

Now that we've cooperated with you, please release some of the hostages.

Alex yelled and said: You'll only get dead bodies out of this stadium!!! Now, you have 2 hours to prepare that plane and get 10 buses here stat.

Jim asked: What do you want ten buses for?

Alex replied: We're taking some of the hostages with us and you have to prepare a green zone for our flight to Panama. Once we get there safely, we'll give you the bomb's deactivation code and free the hostages.

Jim asked: Why should I believe a word you're saying?

Alex laughed and said: I don't have to convince you of anything. Once you're time is up you'll realize who you're talking to. But I wouldn't risk playing with peoples' lives like that if I were you. If you call and inform me that everything is ready before your time runs out, we're good. Otherwise, you'll realize how big of a mistake you've made. I'll be waiting.
Jim reported back to the President.

The President said: Let's wait for this creature and see what it can do. You go prepare the bus but if they get on the plane and we don't do anything, the city will be destroyed and a bunch of innocent people will die.

Ratin and Mitra arrived at the stadium and called Alec and he opened the way for their car to pass. After getting into the car with them he said hello and asked whether the Diamond Man was there as well.

The Diamond Man replied: I'm here. Of course you already knew that.

Alec said: You're right. I might not be that bright but you better be if you want to save all those people.

Then they got into a van which was the operation headquarters of the negotiating team. Jim kicked everybody out except those accompanying the

Diamond Man. He then said: Well, where's this extraordinary creature everyone's talking about.

Ratin replied: He's sitting right next to me sir.

But Jim couldn't see him so the Diamond Man made himself visible.

Jim was shocked and said: This is great! You can make yourself invisible and this is the best thing we could have asked for.

The President and Secretary of Defense joined them via teleconferencing. The

President said: So, you're the famous Diamond Man. How can you help us?

The Diamond Man replied: I can make myself invisible and help you with the rescue operation.

The Secretary of Defense explained the mission: We have to find out exactly how many remote controls there are and the best time to find this out and figure out who their leader exactly is, when they are in the plane.

Everybody agreed with this plan and it was decided that the Diamond Man would be set into action once the terrorists leave the stadium.

The President said: I hope this works. It's our only chance and we better get lucky.

Jim informed every one of the cameras and the listening devices that were set up in the plane and how they could follow the terrorists' every move with them. He also pointed out the fact that the entire crew were part of the SWAT team. Then he turned to the Diamond Man and said: Your job is to figure out, first hand, who their leader is, how many bomb controls there are, and who's carrying them. By the time we try to figure out this information on our own it'll be too late that's why we're counting on you to do it.

The Diamond Man replied: Don't worry about it. I'll be very careful.

Then Jim showed the Diamond Man where each camera would be and how they would be in contact.

Fernanda called Ratin and informed him that they had left the city and asked where Ratin and Mitra were. Ratin told her that they were safe. Everything was set for the operation to take place and the buses were parked in front of the stadium with the President's command. Then, Jim called Alex and informed him that the buses were ready and the plane had been arranged as well. Once again, Alex threatened that they would have to pay a big price if anything went wrong once the terrorists set foot out of the stadium. Everyone was under a lot of pressure and stress over how they would control the situation and what would happen to the hostages.

After a couple of minutes a bunch of the terrorists, who were wearing anti-chemical masks and carrying guns exited the stadium along with a bunch of hostages whose feet were locked with chains. It was a terrifying site and the cameras were reporting everything as it happened.

Jim turned to his group and said:

If only I knew which one of them was in charge I would order an attack on them right now. But my hands are tied.

Then he turned to the Diamond Man and continued:

You're our only hope!

The Diamond Man made himself invisible and blended into the crowd. After an hour or so the buses were filled with the hostages.

Jim said: It's too bad that we can't identify any of the prisoners, terrorists or even the head of the group. They've blended into the crowd. They may have even hidden themselves amongst the hostages so that we wouldn't suspect them.

The buses started moving. The Diamond Man skipped the roofs of each bus looking for the person who was in charge until he heard a voice from one of the buses that was saying:

Sir, do you REALLY think there's a plan waiting for us?

Someone replied: I hope so, otherwise we'll have to take action according to the plan.

The Diamond Man guessed that the second man should be the head of the terrorists but there was nothing he could do until they got the airport.

The police was guiding the buses towards the airport when Alex said: Guys! We did it! They've prepared a plan for us. Victory is ours!

Then they all got out of the bus and into the plane. The Diamond Man followed Alex everywhere he went. Then he carefully followed him onto the plane. There were about 400 people on the plane but nobody knew who the real hostages were. The police couldn't follow their every move and once the doors of the plane were closed the terrorists were happy that they had made it. But there happiness scared the hostages even more. Once the order for take -off came the plane flew to the skies. Now, the Diamond Man was the only person who could save everyone. Alex and a bunch of the terrorists under his command went to the pilot's cockpit while the others stood guard on the first floor. The Diamond Man started wandering around when he overheard a conversation between one of the terrorists and Alex.

The terrorist asked: Sir, when are you going to blow up the stadium?

Alex replied: I haven't decided yet, maybe when we arrive in Panama safe and sound.
When Jim and his team heard this they asked the President for permission to blow up the plane.

The President said: Why would you want to do something like that? Jim told the President about the last conversation they had heard between the terrorists. The President was terrified and said: Have you found the control of the bombs yet? Are you certain there isn't a separate control in the stadium?
Jim had no answer so the President decided to wait and see what the Diamond Man would do.

The Diamond Man was on the first floor and had decided to start his operation. He went towards the resting area where 3 terrorists were seated. He started playing with the bathroom which attracted the attention of one of the three. Once the other two left that part of the plane the Diamond Man attacked the terrorist who was there and killed him and dragged his body to the bathroom. Then he copied his voice and called out his friend to go and see something unusual which was there. He then killed the second terrorist as well. Using the same technique he killed five of the terrorists by breaking their necks. The resting lounge was no longer a safe spot for the terrorists and once the SWAT team saw each of them die on the monitor they screamed and jumped up and down with excitement. It was a stressful time and everyone was praying that the bodies in the bathroom wouldn't be discovered. Jim started talking with the Diamond Man via one of the microphone they had placed in the bathroom. He asked him to break the bathroom door so no one would find the bodies. Then he ordered the Diamond Man to go one of the bathrooms whenever he needed to contact them. Jim also informed him that Alex is in the cockpit and his right-hand man is in the kitchen eating and that each has a remote in their hands and all the Diamond Man had to do was to get a hold of those controls. As he was saying this, suddenly, he was informed that there's another control in the stadium. He asked the Diamond Man to be very careful. The Diamond Man followed Jim's orders one by one. Then he went towards the cockpit and despite the fact that two men were guarding the door, the Diamond Man knocked on it. The two men stared at each other wondering whether one of them had accidently knocked the door when Alex came out and yelled at them for bothering him. As he was yelling, the Diamond Man carefully slipped into the cockpit and when the door was closed, Alex contacted his right-hand man and told him that he would blow up the stadium once they arrived in Panama. Everyone was terrified and Jim prayed that the Diamond Man could do something.

After he finished talking, Alex was about to lit a cigar when the Diamond Man quickly attacked him and broke his neck. Before the bodyguard could do anything, he was killed and well and the pilots who couldn't see anything were terrified.

The Diamond Man said: Don't be alarmed. I'm harmless.
Then he made himself visible and the two pilots said:
So, you're the famous Diamond Man.

The Diamond Man asked: Do you know me?

The pilots replied: We're part of the SWAT team and we were told that you would come to our rescue. We're glad to finally meet you up close.

The Diamond Man said: It's nice work alongside such brave men!
Jim called and thanked them via the speaker and then asked the Diamond Man to go and find the rest of the two remaining remote controls.
Suddenly, the co-pilot said:
But what if they contact us?! Their boss is head! What should we do.

The Diamond Man asked for a recording device and the pilot gave him his cell phone. The Diamond Man mimicked Alex's voice and said:
Stop calling me! I'll contact you whenever I need you! Everything is fine up here! Keep a watch and wait for my call.

The pilot was surprised and told the Diamond Man to go. He ensured him that he would play the recording if any of the terrorists tried to contact their leader. Once the Diamond Man left, the captain locked the door from inside.

The Diamond Man went into the kitchen and noticed how the remote was on the table and the right-hand man was eating. So, he slowly took the remote and killed the right-hand man. The other three terrorists who were in the room didn't understand what was going on and drew their guns and yelled. The Diamond Man quickly killed them all. The sound of shooting had scared the passengers. The Diamond Man also slammed the other terrorists to the wall and took their guns and started shooting towards them. The passengers were terrified and took shelter under their seats. All they could see were two guns dangling in the air and shooting. Everyone was wondering who was shooting.

One of the terrorists yelled: Who's shooting us?!!!! How is it that we can't see him?

The Diamond Man made himself visible and said:
Cowards! It's me!

They all started shooting him but the bullet had no effect on his body. He laughed and shot them until he ran out of bullets. He attacked them and they all ran away. He started flying above their heads and killed one of them. They all ran towards the first floor and those who were on the first floor started shooting the Diamond Man again. Then he took one of their guns and killed a bunch of them. Once a bunch of the terrorists were killed the rest begged for mercy and surrendered. The Diamond Man asked some of the people to tie them up and went back to the cockpit and the pilot opened the door for him. He went in and informed Jim that he had taken complete control of the plan. When asked what he had done with the second control, the Diamond Man returned to the kitchen and picked it up from the trash bin and went back to the cockpit. Everyone was happy and Ratin said to Mitra: I'm glad he was able to get hold of the two controls!

Mitra asked: How do these controls work from such a distance?

Ratin replied: I think they're satellite based.
As they were discussing this someone called the plane and asked whether all was well there. The Diamond Man mimicked Alex's voice and said:
Good going! Wait for my orders!
Jim ordered the pilot to go back to the airport. Although the prison warden wanted to know how many prisoners had been killed, Jim could not give him an exact number. With Jim's order, the Diamond Man exited the plane from under the wheels and flew to the stadium. He arrived at the location of the SWAT team after a couple of minutes.

Everyone thanked him and the necessary arrangements were made for him to enter the stadium and get the third bomb remote control. Suddenly, there was a call from the stadium which was connected to the SWAT room. The Diamond Man picked up, according to

plan and said: Change of plans! You have to exit the stadium with the remote control in your hand. I've arranged a car for you. Wait there till I inform you of the location you have to go to. The city has been evacuated. No one will suspect you. Don't inform anyone until you hear back from me.

The SWAT team set up a black van in a street next to the stadium and took control of it. They evaluated their strategy one more time and then informed the Diamond Man. They called the stadium and the Diamond Man took over:

Take exit 2 and go towards the sewers. Once you reach the street next to the stadium, you'll see a black van. Get in and wait for my orders. Do not inform anyone. You're the only one who knows of this plan!

The terrorist asked: We can all exit together! Why wait?

The Diamond Man replied: You idiot! If you all leave at the same time you might get caught! You go first and once you're out of the woods call me with the cell phone I've placed in the car and I will tell you what to do next. Avoid telling your friends so they won't suspect anything, otherwise you might get killed! Be careful!

The terrorist turned to one of his men and said:
Be on the look-out and if the boss calls tell him I went to the bathroom. He went to the bathroom, found the sewers and took them to get to the street where he found the car. He took a look around and once he was sure the car was empty he got in put the remote control next to his feet and started looking for the cell phone. At that moment the Diamond Man, who was sitting in the front seat reappeared and the terrorist was scared to death and couldn't move a muscle. I was about to escape when he was hit on the head, thrown out of the car and arrested by the SWAT team. Then the SWAT team and the Diamond man used the same route to get to the stadium. Then they called the stadium and the Diamond Man spoke to the forces in the caught terrorists voice and said:
Something suspicious is going on in the parking lot. Five of you stay in the stadium and the rest come to the parking.

One of the terrorists asked: Why?

The Diamond Man replied: You idiot! Stop asking questions! Just follow order or you'll be arrested. Inform the others of this new decision.

There were 26 terrorists stationed in the stadium, 21 of which moved towards the parking lot. They arrived at the parking lot at the same time that the Diamond Man arrived at the stadium. Once they got in the parking lot door shot closed behind them and they were surrounded by the SWAT team and the officer in charge said:

Surrender!

They started shooting at the police. At the same time, the Diamond Man got to the stadium and hit one of the terrorist from behind and he fell to the ground. The audience was surprised and had no idea what was going on. The Diamond Man made himself visible for a minute and while people were frightened at first, they then realized what was going on and were happy that they were about to be set free. The Diamond Man handed the terrorist's gun to one of the people and asked them to watch him while he took care of the others. Once the Diamond Man got to the second terrorist he called him and when he turned around he was punched so hard that he went up in the air and fell back down where the players started beating him with their hockey sticks. Although one of the hostages got a hold of his gun the other two remaining terrorists started shooting at the Diamond Man. The Diamond Man took those two men and flew up in the sky and then let them go. The SWAT team had also killed a bunch of the terrorists and arrested the rest. The bomb defusing team entered the stadium and the hostages were able to leave from the two exits.

There were a lot of bombs that were easily defused except one which was placed under a big column. Once they touched it a recording said:

You think you're so clever but our boss is cleverer than you!

The bomb turned on and the timer showed 10 minutes. The bomb defusing

team contact Jim and said: We can't risk it. Although I should say that none of these bombs are chemical.

Jim asked: Now, what do we do?

The bomb defusing team suggested:

We have to take the bomb somewhere safe and let it explode because there's no way we can defuse it.

Jim suggested: I know the perfect place. It's an abandoned underground mine.

I gave the location of the mine to the Diamond Man. He took the bomb and quickly flew there. Two helicopters escorted him. There was one minute remaining on the bomb clock when he threw it into the mine and came out waiting for it to explode. Suddenly, he saw an old man who was trying to lit a fire in front of the mine. He quickly flew down and picked him up. The old man was scared and started screaming for help, when he heard the bomb explode and everywhere turned bright. The helicopters which were near the site stood in their place till the explosion subsided. The Diamond Man handed the old man over to the helicopters and flew back to the stadium while one of the helicopters landed to assess the situation.

Everyone was enjoying a victory they never imagined. Jim thanked everyone and said:

Although we weren't able to arrest all of the terrorists, we succeeded in saving people's lives.

The President also talked with the nation on TV and thanked everyone and promised to further investigate the matter.

The city was safe once again. Mitra was hugging the Diamond Man and crying with joy when Alec approached them and said:

Your home will no longer be under surveillance. We are proud of you.

They were happy to hear the great news and called their friends. Sofia informed them that they were stuck in traffic trying to get back home and asked them to go home and rest and they would meet the next day. On the way back home Mitra complimented the Diamond Man on his ability to copy people's voices and wondered whether he would be able to freely wonder about the city, now that everyone knew about him. Ratin said they had to ask the officials. When they got home, they ran into their neighbor David. He apologized and said he was merely worried and had no intention of interfering in their lives. Ratin and Mitra forgave him and actually thanked him because he had helped the Diamond Man gain a more free life and given him the ability to be able to help all those people. They invited David in for a cup of Persian tea but he thanked him and postponed it to another night when they would be his guest in order for a better apology to be made. Mitra made some tea and they all laid down on the sofas talking about how famous the Diamond Man had become and joking about getting his autograph before it was too late. After tea, they went to bed and the Diamond Man laid down in front of the TV.

The next day Fernanda called and informed them that they would be coming over with their kids this time since everyone knew the Diamond Man now and was curious to meet him. In the afternoon, when the guests arrived, their kids were excited to meet the Diamond Man and easily became friends with him. The grown-ups talked about what had happened the other day and Ratin called the officials who gave permission for the Diamond Man to freely walk about the streets as long as he avoids attracting too much attention to himself. So, Ratin gave the Diamond Man new clothes but no longer made him wear a mask or gloves and they all went to a restaurant for dinner.

Once they got to the restaurant everyone wanted to take pictures with the Diamond Man and his friends. Everyone was glad that they could finally easily bring the Diamond Man out. The restaurant owner went to their table and informed them that, that night's dinner was on the house and he replied that it was a small token to thank the hero who had saved the city. After dinner they all went home and as usual the Diamond Man sat in front of the TV. Mitra came in with a cup of tea and asked about the latest news. It was still all about what had happened the other day and how interrogations of the remaining terrorists were going. There was also a piece of news about Columbia and how some smugglers had managed to smuggle people and drugs across the border, attacking villages and taking the entire villagers as hostage. This had been done before and the villagers would be taken for forced labor on poppy farms and labor camps. The government could not fight them and the people had been taken to an undisclosed location. Some interviews with the Columbian people were also broadcasted. This piece of news disappointed the Diamond man greatly and he asked where Columbia was. Mitra brought a globe and pointed to Columbia. The Diamond Man asked for permission to go there and help the people but Ratin found such a suggestion to be too dangerous but the Diamond Man insisted on going even if they wouldn't help him. Ratin suggested that they contact Daniel, who was from Brazil, and had a lot of friends in South America to gain more information. Ratin called Daniel and asked him to come to their home the next day so they could go to work together.

The next morning when Daniel arrived, the Diamond Man greeted him and Ratin told him what they were planning. Daniel promised to ask some of his friends to see if they could give him the exact location of the smugglers. Before Mitra could bring anything for him Daniel left and decided to skip work that day so he could meet up with some people and ask about the smugglers whereabouts.

Six days went by and the Diamond Man would go to NASA headquarters every day and undergo some tests and then come back home in the afternoon and then they'd go out and have fun with their friends. Until Daniel's friends found some traces of the smugglers and he gave Ratin and Mitra the whereabouts. Since they couldn't just hop on a plan and leave the country Daniel suggested that they use one of his friends' personal jet but they decided to leave over the weekend since the Diamond Man had to go to NASA every day. Daniel said that he would set everything up for their trip.

A week went by and the weekend came. Daniel called and informed them that the plane would be ready for departure at 8pm. Daniel himself and Franco joined them for the trip. Once they got to the airport, Daniel asked the Diamond Man to make himself disappear and go to the Lane four where the plane that would take them to Columbia was waiting. After seven hours of flying , they reached an airport in the middle of a jungle where Daniel's friends were waiting to greet them. They drove for two hours and then their guide told them that they had to walk the rest since they were close to the smugglers location they had to hide the cars with leaves and move. They learned of the exact location on a map and set out. After a couple minutes of walking, the Diamond Man said:

It's too dangerous for you guys. I'll take you to the top of the trees so if anyone comes you won't be seen.

Once he helped them all get up the tree, he continued:

This is the first time I'm volunteering to do something. Wish me luck!

He then made himself invisible and left. When he got to the first security stop he thought to himself: "I don't want to be invisible this time." So he made himself visible again and shouted out to the napping guards:

You lazy heads! Are you napping or standing guard?

They woke up and were terrified at the sight of him and started shooting at him. He hid behind a tree and then came out and approached them. They started shooting again. This time the Diamond Man said:

Seems that you don't speak English! It doesn't matter anyway because these are your last breaths.

One by one he took them each down but the shooting noise had attracted attention. Some of the forces came towards the first guard post and started shooting at him but since he kept flying from side to side, they couldn't get him. The Diamond Man left for the base fort where he was greeted with heavy shooting. Finally, their commander woke up and realized they had been attacked but the question was by whom.

One of the forces spoke: Sir, we don't know who has attacked us.

The commander asked:

You mean all this shooting is for one person?!!!!

The soldier replied: Yes, sir. But he's an unusual creature that flies.

The commander yelled: Then what are you good for nothings doing? Kill him immediately! I had just fallen asleep. You ruined my day!

The commander was still drunk from the previous night so he went back to his room. The Diamond Man kept flying around and everyone was shooting at him. He went towards one of the guard poles and kicked three of the guards down and started shooting towards the others. A bunch of the smugglers were injured. One of the smugglers shot a bazooka towards the Diamond Man but he was careful and quickly flied up and the Bazooka hit one of the poles, destroying it completely. The explosion woke the commander and he realized how grave the situation really was so he took a gun and called out to his bodyguards:

What the heck is going on here? Who are you shooting at? I can't see anyone.

One of his bodyguards pointed to the Diamond Man, who was flying above.

The commander couldn't think right and thought he might still be asleep and started shooting at the Diamond Man. The Diamond Man went from pole to pole killing the people in each pole and throwing them down. Another person shot with a bazooka at him but he wasn't hurt and instead took the bazooka and started shooting himself. He shot at the commander's headquarters. Everywhere was full of chaos. Then, he discovered their arms warehouse. Once another bazooka was shot the entire warehouse exploded and a bunch of people were killed. All workers who were packaging the illegal drugs ran away and attacked their bosses and got their hands on the guns and attacked the prison guards. The commander who noticed how messed up everything was turned to his bodyguards and said:

Get in the car! We'll head towards the secret hiding place.

But once they got into the car a bunch of the prisoners noticed them and attacked their car, killing a bunch of the heads of the smugglers. Additionally, the Diamond Man shot the containers of illegal drugs and after half an hour the hostages and workers had taken control of the base. The Diamond Man had succeeded in helping release innocent people. They all hailed him and he took a spin and went back to join his friends. He brought them down from the tree. They had been sick worried since they had heard a lot of shooting but the Diamond Man ensured them that all was well and they decided to quickly leave the premises. The guide thanked them for their help and they got on a plane and left for L.A. Everyone was tired and took a nap on the way back but the Diamond Man took some time to enjoy the view until they reached their destination at night.

The next day all the news broadcasts talked of the smuggling base in Columbia and how it had been freed of the smugglers and everyone was talking of an unusual creature that looked like glass and had helped them while flying overhead. All the people who were interviewed praised him and the recordings which were taken by disclosed cameras on the grounds showed videos and everyone found out that it was the Diamond Man who had saved the Columbians.

The security forces called them in and interrogated them. Ratin informed them that the Diamond Man, himself, wanted to help those people but the interrogator was hard on them and said they were not allowed to do anything without proper permission from the security forces and the government. The President was informed of the matter but he ordered them to be freed with a warning to inform the officials the next time they want to do something like that. The interrogator informed them of the President's decision and threatened them that they wouldn't be so easy on them next time. The Diamond Man didn't pay attention to his threats and warned that he could do whatever he wanted and that no one could stop him.

When the interrogator heard this he said:
I might not be able to touch you but I can always arrest your friends.
The Diamond Man stood up and took up by the throat and raised him from the ground and hit him to the wall saying:
Threaten my friends one more time and you'll have to answer to me!
The other forces came in to help and attacked the Diamond Man but he hit them all with his other hand and pushed them back. Finally, Ratin interfered to cool things down. The inspector threatened to report everything but they

ignored him and Ratin said: You can't do anything! He's a national hero!
They all left and the front door guards were told to let them pass.
At home the Diamond Man apologized for his behavior and said he just wanted to protect his friends.

Mitra replied: I know but you have to understand that if anyone were to take matters into his/her own hands than we would no longer be safe.

The Diamond Man replied: You're right. I'll try to be more careful from now on. But, at least, they learned to not mess with me!
They all laughed.

A couple days later, one night when they were all watching TV and talking and having fun with their friends until the news came one and the Diamond Man asked them all to be quieter. One of the headlines read: 'An unusual discovery in "Burned City" of Iran'. They waited to hear the complete news and finally they learned that in Burned City near Zabol in Iran a glass statue of a women along with some other glass objects were found. They all stared at each other and the Diamond Man was excited to learn more. Once the news was over, Mitra who had recorded that bit said:

Let's watch it again!
When they got to the part where the statue was shown they paused and stared at the image comparing it with the Diamond Man.

The Diamond Man said: It looks just like me!

Ratin agreed and said: How could it be! In Iran, in the Burned City! A thousand year old creature that looks just like you! I can't wrap my head around it!

Sofia added: What does this mean? It's unbelievable! Why should there be a statue that looks exactly like you in such an ancient place! Does this mean they had some kind of contact with your people?

Mitra said: Maybe they were! Otherwise, how could they be so similar?!

Ratin suggested: We have to look into this!

Mitra suggested that they take the film on a flash drive to the authorities in the research facility. The Diamond Man was still in awe and said:
It looks exactly like me! How could it be! What must have happened in that city? I'd like to know more.

Mitra said: We can learn more here. Iran is one of the most ancient countries in the world and its full of ancient hills that are over seven thousand years old which have not been completely studied yet like the Silk Hills in Kashan which have been there for 8000 years. Iran is full of historical secrets!

Mitra took him to the computer and once they were connected to the internet, she googled 'Burned City'. A bunch of information and pictures of that location came up which she showed the Diamond Man. They went back to their friends after half an hour of web surfing. Sofia asked: Did you find out anything about the 'Burned City'?

The Diamond Man replied: It's fascinating! They had brain surgery! They built fake eyes! They built the world's oldest dice for Backgammon and the drew the oldest animation on a clay plates. I also saw a goat that jumped up a tree and took a leaf. They had water pipes and most interesting of all no weapons were found in the 'Burned City'. Additionally, 12 different types of fabric were found there and a painting on a piece of leather.

Sofia said: Good job memorizing all those things!

The Diamond Man replied: These are just a small portion of the things that we found.

Sofia replied: We know! We love Iranian history and we've learned all about it before!

The Diamond Man asked: How?

Sofia replied: Because we have two Iranian researchers who love history called Ratin and Mitra.

They all laughed then the Diamond Man said: With all this information I got regarding the 'Burned City' I can't wait to find out what's going on there.

Franco said: It takes time and you have to be patient.

Fernanda added: Can't wait to see what will happen tomorrow!
They all had lunch and parted ways. The next morning Ratin and Mitra headed to the research center and handed the video of the news they had heard to the head of the research team, Michael. He called in some of the employees and they all watched. When it was over, Mitra asked: What do you think?

Michael replied:
I'm not sure. We have to conduct some more studies. Surely, Iran is a country with a rich historical background and we shouldn't be surprised that such a thing would show up there.

He then turned to the Diamond Man and said: Come with me. We'll take some pictures of you and make some comparisons, see what we can find.

The next couple of days were spent on taking similar picture of the Diamond Man and comparing it with those artifacts found in 'Burned City'. On the 21st day of the studies when they went to the research facility after a couple of minutes the vice president, Allen, came in and said:

Sir, I've got great news! I've just received an email from my friend in Italy informing me that the diamond statue will be transferred to Italy for further investigations and it will arrive in 10 days.

The Diamond Man exclaimed: What wonderful news! Thank you!

Michael said: We have to start planning our trip to Italy. I'll inform the security officials and make the necessary arrangements. That's enough for today.

They called Ratin and told him he could come, pick up the Diamond Man.

Once he arrived Ratin asked: Why did you finish early today?

The Diamond Man replied: I have big news my friend!

Ratin asked: What is it?

The Diamond Man replied: Guess. Ratin continued:Have you discovered a new form of power in yourself?

The Diamond Man replied: Nope. They're taking me to a military base tomorrow so they can see how well I can function.

Ratin said: That's great!

The Diamond Man continued: But that's not all!

Ratin asked: What else?

The Diamond Man answered: I'll tell you when we get home! I have to tell both you and Mitra at the same time! I can't wait!
As hard as Ratin tried to get a word out of him, the Diamond Man insisted that he wouldn't say anything until they get home and se Mitra.
He said to Ratin:
Honey, be patient!

Ratin laughed and said:
You've mastered our language. You're becoming more and more like us! You may even turn into a human one day!

The Diamond Man laughed and said: Or you may turn into diamonds like me!

They joked about it for a while until they got home. Mitra wasn't back from work so Ratin called her and asked if she could come home earlier than usual since the Diamond Man had something to say. While they were waiting for her to arrive, Ratin made tea and they were watching TV when Mitra got home!

Ratin brought her a cup of tea and said:

Well, Mitra is here! Now, will you tell us what's going on?

The Diamond Man said: I want you to guess.

But Mitra replied: I really don't know. Please tell us!

The Diamond Man said: Fine! I'll tell you! The statue of the glass women will be sent to Italy in the next ten days for further research.

Mitra screamed of joy and hugged Ratin and said: That's incredible news! Now, what do we do?

The Diamond Man said: Michael told me that they would make the necessary arrangements with Italy so we can all go there.

Mitra exclaimed: That's wonderful! I can't wait to see that statue up close! What about you?

Ratin added: I'm super excited too!

The Diamond Man also said: I can't believe I'm going to get to see that statue which I wanted from up close.

They decided to celebrate that night with their friends. As usual, everyone came to Ratin and Mitra's house and then left for the restaurant. When Franco asked what the occasion was Mitra told them that they learn about it once they get to the restaurant. They ordered red wine at the restaurant and Fernanda asked:

Well, what's going on? What's your big news?

Mitra made them guess. One of them guessed that something new had come up with the Diamond Man while another guessed that Mitra and Ratin were going to have a baby.

Franco said: Are you planning a trip?

Mitra replied: The last one was close but where to?

Daniel replied: It's a small world we can go anywhere we want. Wait, is there gonna be another special operation?

Mitra said: You lose! Now I'll tell you what's going on. The statue of the glass women which was found in Iran is going to be in Italy in 10 days and we are going to go there with the Diamond Man to participate in the research process.

Sofia said: That's great news! So, that's why we're celebrating tonight! They all turned to the Diamond Man and asked him how he was feeling. He expressed joy over getting to do what he wanted all along. Finally, they parted ways after dinner.

On the way home, Ratin told the Diamond Man:

You'll be going to a different facility tomorrow for new exams to be made. How do you feel?

The Diamond Man replied:

Well, to tell you the truth I have some powers that you haven't seen yet.

-Like what? Ratin asked.

The Diamond Man replied: Like shooting hard diamonds out of my bare hands.

Ratin stopped the car and said: This isn't a busy street shoot at that tree. Let's see what you got!

The Diamond Man put his hand out of the car, made a fist, and turned it towards the tree. His hand turned yellow and then red.

Ratin said: Your hand looks like lava!

Suddenly, some small pieces were fired from the Diamond Man's hand and hit the tree. Ratin jumped out of the car and drew one of them out of the tree and said:

It's extremely hard, just like a diamond.

Then he showed it to Mitra. She said:

I think it IS diamond! But I'll have to show to an expert.

The Diamond Man explained:If I want to I can make the diamonds reattach to my body.

Ratin asked him to try to do it. The Diamond Man made an attempt and all the pieces that had been fired including the one Mitra had taken were reattached to his body.

Mitra said: I was enjoying that piece of diamond!

The Diamond Man placed his hand above hers and returned a piece to her. She asked:

You did that so slowly and gently. How could you control the speed?

The Diamond Man replied:

It depends on the distance between my hand and the object I want to shoot at. I can control the speed and intensity.

Mitra asked: How is it that your hand turned red the first time you shot the diamonds but not the second time?

The Diamond Man replied: It's because I haven't used such power in a really long time.

Ratin asked: Why haven't you used it in the recent events?

The Diamond Man replied: There was no need. I merely used their own weapons and my other weapon which is turning invisible which I don't like to use when I'm fighting.

Ratin asked: What other powers do you have?

The Diamond Mans said: The less you know the better.
Mitra agreed. Ratin continued:
You're right. You should keep this hidden in the next tests as well. Otherwise, we'll never hear the end of it.

The Diamond Man agreed and said: I wasn't sure which aspects of my abilities I should show.

Ratin told him: All you have to show them is how you become invisible and fly. They don't need to know the rest.
The Diamond Man agreed. Mitra asked him why he had shown this other special power to them.

The Diamond Man replied:You're my dear friends and my family. You're different. I'll do anything to keep you happy and I would never allow anyone to hurt you.

Ratin said: We love you too and we're glad that you've become part of our family. We'd do anything to keep you safe.

Mitra said: Let's go. It's really quiet here. Someone might suspect us.

In the morning Ratin dropped off the Diamond Man at the research center and went to work. The military research revealed the fact that his body was bullet proof and anti-radar. They also tested his ability to fly and move about. They set up a bunch of maneuvers for him with airplanes and helicopters.

The chief commander was impressed with such abilities and said:

I've never seen such great ability to fly. Nothing can catch up to him. He also has the ability to turn invisible whenever he wishes. With such flying skills and an anti-radar body we can use him in all sorts of undercover operations.

In the after Ratin picked him up as usual. The Diamond Man told him everything and explained how the chief commander was planning on using him in all sorts of operations. Ratin said:

It was a good idea to hide your other abilities from them. It'll be easier for you this way.

A few days went by till they heard that the necessary coordination for the Italy trip had been made and they would be travelling there soon to study both the Diamond Man and the glass woman. A few days later they were all on a plane to Italy. The Diamond Man turned to Ratin and said:

I'm glad you could join me. Sorry for disrupting your work schedules.

Ratin said: Don't worry about it. Daniel and Franco have everything under control at the firm and Sofia and Fernanda are taking care of the gym. We're glad that we could join you. Not only because we get to accompany you but also because this statue was found in OUR country which makes this trip more interesting than ever.

Once they arrived at the airport, they were transferred to an undisclosed location in special cars. The next day, after having breakfast they were taken to the main hall. Everyone was amazed at the site of the Diamond Man. Different people from different parts of the site had come to see them. Finally, they reached room A which was the research headquarters on the Iranian statue. The head of the research center, Mr. Alberto, came forward and welcomed them. Then he turned to the Diamond Man and said:

I saw the statue a couple days ago and now a live version of it is standing in front of me. You two truly resemble one another.

The Diamond Man said: I can't wait to see this statue.

Mr. Alberto said: Then I won't keep you waiting.

Then he led them to a room. Mr. Alberto said:

Here's the statue that you've been dying to see!

The Diamond Man ran in, went towards the statue and looked at it carefully. It was facing downwards on a bed. He was so absolved in watching it that he forgot all about the people around him who also wanted to see the statue. He was just walking around it very fast and examining it from every angle.

One of the members of the American team said: Could you please move so we can take a look as well?

The Diamond Man couldn't hear a word. Michael turned to his team and said:

Let him look all he wants. He's the one who has to do all the looking right now. We can wait.

After a couple of minute the Diamond Man turned to Mitra and said:

I can't believe how an ancient civilization has been able to build such a thing! How is it possible? It's like looking in a mirror! Oh, excuse me I didn't mean to keep you waiting. I was merely distracted.

Ratin said: It's okay. You're the main person that needs to see this.

The American team went forward and was amazed at how similar the statue and the Diamond Man were. After half an hour of examining the statue and discussing the similarities, they were set to begin their studies. The Diamond Man was taken for a 3D scan of his entire body to be made. After a couple of hours, all of the images of both the statue and the Diamond Man were ready. Everyone gathered in the main room and placed the pictures next to one another focusing on the details of sizes. Both were of the same size and measures and the more they studied each of them they more they realized how similar they are. It was decided that they would sample some parts of the Diamond Man to compare with that of the statue but they weren't sure how this could be done. The Diamond Man told them that he had given Mitra a piece of his body and she took it from her bag and handed it to Alberto. They asked how he had detached it from himself. The Diamond Man said: I have my ways!

Alberto said:You're right and it's to our advantage because sampling your body would have been a great challenge for us.

The Diamond Man asked: Then how are you going to sample the statue?

Alberto replied: Well, we can't detach anything from it so we'll have to resort to other ways to examine it. That way we can examine its tissues. But since you're very much alive we can sample your body which increases the speed of our studies.

Paula, who was the photographer of the team, asked the Diamond Man:

Where were you before you came to Earth? Tell us more about your past.

Ratin said: We've asked him before but he doesn't remember. All he remembers is that he was on the moon and he would see the Earth from up there, but he doesn't remember anything else.

Paula said: That's too bad. It would have helped us greatly if we knew where he had come from. Now that we finally have an alien, he can't remember anything about where he is from so we can't contact the others.
After two hours, they were given a break and the Diamond Man asked if he could take a walk and look around.

Alberto said: Be my guest. But please come back in half an hour so we can continue.

Mitra asked if he wanted them to join him but he said he wanted to be alone so Mitra and Ratin went to have a cup of coffee and the Diamond Man went from room to room looking around till he ran into four janitors. They didn't notice him. One of them was upset and the others were trying to cheer him up. The Diamond Man was curious and stopped to learn what was going on. The man was crying and talking in Arabic:
I told you these smugglers couldn't be trusted. But you insisted.

The Diamond Man went close and asked: What's wrong?

They all turned quiet. The men kept crying and asked:

Are you that alien everyone is talking about?

The Diamond Man replied: Yes, you speak English very well. What's wrong?

What's your name? The main replied: I'm Foad.

The Diamond Man asked: Are you Arab?

Foad replied: Yes. I spent all my money on trying to smuggle my family from Libya and bringing them here but now I've been informed that the person who was going to put them on a boat and bring them here is going to kill everyone on board and throw them into the ocean.

The Diamond Man asked: Then why didn't you friend inform them of such plans so they wouldn't board the ship?

Foad replied: He tried but they had already gone and I don't know which ship it going to bring them. They leave no traces of themselves. They've set out a day earlier than planned.

As they were talking his cell phone rang and he said: It's from Libya. Everyone was quiet. He talked for a couple of minutes and then hung up and said:

They've set out on a white ferry that has black line and has the Italian flag drawn on it. It might be too late.

He started crying again. The Diamond Man was very upset and said: Don't worry. I'll help you.

Foad asked: How can you help me? These people are really dangerous and we don't even know where they are.

The Diamond Man replied: You let me worry about the dangers. I can handle it.

Foad asked: How are you going to get there?

The Diamond Man replied:

I can fly very fast I just need a map.

Foad said: There's a big map in one of the rooms. Come with me and I'll show you.

The Diamond Man asked how well they had learned English rather than Italy and they told him that they had learned English when they were back in their own country. Finally, they found the map.

The Diamond man asked Foad to show him where the port was and in which direction it was headed towards Italy. Foad showed him the locations on the map.

The Diamond Man asked: Where are we now?

Foad showed Rome on the map. The Diamond Man asked for a compass to find the correct direction. Foad promised to return with one as soon as possible. The Diamond Man asked them to keep the matter under the QT so all would go smoothly. Foad pointed out that it was a long way to go but the Diamond Man was only concerned about saving lives. Faod asked where to give the compass to him, the Diamond Man said:

Put it in a corner in your room and I'll pick it up after hours. Now get back to work. And you come with me to show me where the compass is.

Working hours was up and they were all getting ready to leave.

The Diamond Man asked for permission from Ratin to say good-bye to his friends.

Ratin asked: What friends? Everyone is here!

The Diamond Man said: I befriended some janitors.

Mitra said: That's great! Go ahead!

He ran to the janitor's lounge and picked up the compass and went back.

Ratin asked: What's that in your hand?

The Diamond Man said: I got it from one of my friends,

Ratin said: What an interesting gift! What a great friend!

Mitra said:You're enjoying this, aren't you?

The Diamond Man said: I'm becoming more and more like you guys, especially like Mitra who is full of excitement and funny!

They all laughed and went back to their lounges. After a couple of minutes, he went on the computer and put the location statistics into the computer. He was finally able to find the location, when it turned dark. Mitra went to the shower and Ratin called Franco. The Diamond Man took advantage of this situation, made himself invisible, and flew to the Libyan waters. No one noticed him. He found his way with the help of the compass. He got to where to he wanted in five minutes and looked around in the ports, ships and ferries but couldn't find anything. He went towards a fisherman who got scared and couldn't help him because he was speaking Arabic so he let him go. He kept focusing on the water and took a look at the compass and said to himself:

I can't use this anymore.

So he threw the compass into the water. He opened his arms so he could receive the signals from the ships. Once he got the signals he followed them and went towards two ships, but they weren't the one he was looking for. He did the same with a bunch of other signals but all led him to the wrong ships. Finally, the eighth signal led him to the right ship which was black and white and had an Italian flag on it. He made himself invisible and went towards that ship. A bunch of people were on board who were guarded by armed men. He slowly descended onto the ship and stood in a corner but nothing unusual caught his eye. Suddenly, a bunch of men came out, said some words to each other in Arabic, separated the men and the women and then dragged a women into the room and locked the door. Another man who seemed to be her husband attacked the captain's room but they shot him in the foot. The Diamond Man quickly went to the room and noticed that they were about to rape the women. Although the door was locked the Diamond Man made himself invisible and broke the glass and went in. The smugglers were scared and their boss told them to kill him. Three other men who were there drew their guns and shot at the Diamond Man. He threw all three into the sea. The woman was scared as well but the Diamond Man gave her his hand, picked her up and helped her get out of there. Then he went towards the head of the smugglers and threw him into the sea as well. When the Diamond Man came out, everyone was scared but the women said that he had saved her and is harmless. Another smuggler started shooting at him but they were all thrown into the sea. But suddenly, one of the smugglers took a little girl hostage and

said in Arabic: One step closer and I'll kill her!

The Diamond Man held his arms towards the smuggler and said:

Let her go!

The smuggler started shooting at him and was terrified when he realized the Diamond Man was bullet proof. The Diamond Man shot diamond glasses at him and killed him freeing the little girl. Everyone was dancing about with joy! Suddenly, they heard an explosion from the engine-room which shook the ship and everyone fell down. Then, five armed men came out and started shooting at the Diamond Man. He reacted by shooting them and then he turned to the people on board and asked:

Who here speaks English?

A young man raised his hand and said: I do.

The Diamond Man continued: What's your name?

Bashir. He said. The Diamond Man said:

Ask them if anyone knows how to work a ship.

Bashir repeated the question loudly and in Arabic. Two men raised their hands and came forward. The Diamond Man asked Bashir to tell them to take a look at the motor-house, and he joined them there along with the translator. The body of the ship had holes in it and water was coming in so Bashir said that they had to get the water out of the motor-house and asked the two men:

How's the engine?

Once they took a look at it, they informed him that the engine could no longer be used to move the ship so they went to ask help to get the water off the deck. Some of the men went to help and they took some pieces of wood to cover up the hole which they were able to do after some time. Bashir was there to keep everyone calm. Then the Diamond Man said:

I want to take you to Italy to save you from such a life full of hardship.

Bashir said: But how. It's a long way and the ship can't move without an engine.

The Diamond Man told him that he would make waves that could help the ship move which surprised Bashir given the number of people on board and how heavy the ship was but the Diamond Man was sure he could do it. Once Bashir informed the others of their plans everyone started dancing and laughing. The Diamond Man asked whether anyone had attended to the man who had been shot. Bashir told him that they had patched up his wound using the first aid kit and that he was doing ok for now. The Diamond Man then told him to tell everyone to be prepared and to hold on tight. They helped each other tie the knot. Someone came out of the engine-room and informed them that the body of the ship had been completely fixed.

The Diamond Man said: That's great! Tell everyone to be ready to set sail! We're gonna be moving at maximum speed. Also, tell some of the men to stay in the engine-room in case water gets back in.

The Diamond Man went to the back of the ship and made a small tide with his hands which made the ship slowly move forward. He asked whether they were ready to set sail. Bashir answered yes. Everyone clapped and cheered for the Diamond Man and he increased the intensity of the tides to make the ship go faster. The moon was beautifully shining in the sky.

Back in the base Mitra and Ratin were wondering where the Diamond Man had gone. Mitra suggested that he may be taking to walk around and assured Ratin that he would be back soon and went to work with the computer. When the screen came up she saw all the information that the Diamond Man had looked up regarding Rome and its geographical situation so she asked Ratin:

Honey, why have you been studying the geographical route from Rome to Benghazi? Are you conducting some kind of research?

Ratin answered that he had not looked up such information on the web so Mitra showed it to him. They were both shocked. They connected the dots and guessed that it might have been the Diamond Man's doing since they remembered how he had been talking to the janitors and the compass they had given him.

Mitra said: We'll inform everyone if he's not back in the next hour.
An hour came and there was no sign of the Diamond Man so Ratin and
Mitra informed Michael of his disappearance and he in turn informed
Alberto. Alberto set up a number of search teams and after a couple of
hours they all suspected that he had gone towards the port of Benghazi.
They sent a number of helicopters out into the sea to find him but by
daylight they hadn't found a single trace of the Diamond Man. Finally,
at 4pm one of the helicopters had spotted the ship and the Diamond
Man who was flying behind it guiding them towards the coast. He
immediately informed everyone so they would know that nothing
suspicious had happened.

Everyone was waiting for them at the port and a large number of
reporters were there. Everyone was clapping for him and the Diamond
Man waved to them and flew towards his friends. Alberto and the
American team had also come to greet him. When he arrived Alberto
asked:
How did you know how to find your friends among this large crowd?
The Diamond Man replied:
This is another one of my powers.
Then they all got into a chopper and went back to Rome. On the way
there Ratin asked why the Diamond Man hadn't informed them of his
decision. He said:
I was worried you might not allow me to help those people.

Ratin replied: You should've told us. If we knew innocent lives in danger there's no way we would have stood in your way. Promise me that from now on you will not do anything without letting us know first.

The Diamond Man agreed and they went back. The Italian officials warned him not to take any actions without notifying them and the next day in the interrogation he promised that he wouldn't. They were then moved to a guarded area where the officials could keep a better eye on them. Once they set foot in the research center everyone applauded them and Foad and his friends came forward.

Foad said: Thank you for helping my family get here safely. My brother is done in the ports sorting the necessary paper work so I can bring them home tomorrow. You have given us a new chance to a better life. I will always be indebted to you. I would do anything to make it up to you. .

The Diamond Man wished him and his family the best.

Alberto invited them all to coffee and cake to celebrate the fact that the Diamond Man had saved the lives of all those innocent people and the Diamond Man told them all about how he had attacked the smugglers and saved the people on board. Alberto gave them the day off for what the Diamond Man had done so they all went out in the city to do some sight-seeing.

They continued their stay in Italy for about a week and then they went home but were due back for further research. On the flight back the Diamond Man seemed to have a lot on his mind so Mitra asked what he was thinking about.

The Diamond Man said: You humans are so lucky. There's a vast population of your kind and you know all about how you were born and what goals you have in life. You can get married and do a bunch of other stuff but what about me. I'm all alone and remember nothing of my past. I was so happy to see that statue on TV because I thought it mean I was no longer alone and could finally learn about my past but I was wrong!

Mitra consoled him and said: Don't worry about it! You have us and you're part of our family. We love you and we'd do anything for you. Now let me see that smile! I hate seeing you upset.

The Diamond Man said: You're right. I have to accept the fact that I'm different and I have to lower my expectations. I've lost my memory but I don't know why. I have to get used to living on Earth. Maybe, I'll finally learn the truth about my past someday.
Mitra suggested that they watch a movie on her laptop to lift the Diamond Man's spirits.

At the same time in the Taftan Mountains of Iran a number of workers were working in a rock mine and the chief-miner was guiding the cranes to lead them to where they wanted to cut the rocks. After half an hour, the blade of the crane got stuck in a big rock and although some of the miners tried to free it and turn it back on it only caused some of them to be hurt. The chief-miner ordered them to clean out the rocks by hand to find out what the blade was stuck in. After three hours of hard work, they weren't able to figure out what they had hit so they decided to use dynamites to blow up that specific part and figure out what's underneath. They cleared the space of all personnel and blew up the dynamites. Once the dirt settled, they faced an amazing site and started looking at it.

One of the miners said: We can figure out what it is exactly if we wash out this part.

The chief miner agreed and they used a big water tank to wash down the dirt and stones. After half an hour it was all washed out and they all realized what it was but couldn't believe their eyes. The chief-miner said:

It looks like a space ship. But that's not possible.

One of the workers went on top of it and loudly said:

Wow! Look at this! There are some people here who seem to have died.

Another said:

How could such a person who is stuck under such rubbles stay alive!

One other said: When do you think they got stuck here?

The chief-miner asked: Why are they black and shiny?

One of the miners answered: They may have been burned.

The chief-miner decided to report to the police before matters got out of hand. After a couple hours a couple of police cars as well as some people from the cultural heritage organization came and closed the site. The miners had recorded images of the space ship and put it up on the internet.

On the other hand, Mitra, Ratin and the Diamond Man's plane landed in America. Their friends awaited them in the airport and they all went to Sofia and Franco's house and talked all about the trip.

Three days after their return, the news of what had happened in the Taftan mountains spread throughout the world. One of Mitra's family members sent them videos of it over the web. The video shocked them all and they discussed about the fact that whether they should believe it or not but Mitra said that her family member who had sent it said it was real so they went on the web to verify and noticed how all the other sites were talking about the same thing so they decided to show the video to Michael and Jack the next morning.

The Diamond Man said: I don't really understand what's going on! This whole space ship business has me baffled!

Mitra replied: Me too! It's amazing!

The next morning they all went to the research center and asked to see Michael. Michael came out and said:

We didn't have an appointment for today!

Ratin said: That's not why we're here.

And he handed Michael the videos to watch. There was one part that he needed to be translated and the Diamond Man translated it for him. He exclaimed:

You can speak Farsi???????!!!!!!

The Diamond Man replied: Of course! I live with two Farsi-speakers! How could I not pick it up?

Michael asked: You are very talented! Regarding this space ship business I have to say I can't believe my eyes! What do you guys think?

Ratin said: It's definitely real!

Michael suggested: I have to look into this myself and let you know. By the way, could you email me this video?

Mitra promised to email him the video as soon as possible and then they went home.

On the other hand the cultural heritage officials in Iran took the space ship out of the mine and extracted the bodies from it. A large number of studies were conducted in the mine and the cultural heritage organization bought the whole site as its own property. Two days later, all of this was reported on American news channels and everyone was sure that the spaceship had been stuck in dried up lava which was proven by the shape of the rocks.

The next day weekly research on the Diamond Man resumed and everyone was talking about this new discovery and the six black bodies found in the spaceship. All the videos were double checked.

The Diamond Man said: This is a completely different discovery from that glass statue. These were found in a spaceship stuck in the middle of some lave. What do you guys think?

Michael said: I've already talked to Italy and we'll be sending the six bodies there by the next month for further research.

The Diamond Man felt relieved given that this meant he didn't have to go all the way to Iran himself and see those statues up close.

A couple of minutes later a bunch of national security guards arrived asking to see the Diamond Man. One of them introduced himself as Brian and said he need to have a private conversation with the

Diamond Man on an urgent matter. They went into a room and asked everyone, including Ratin and Mitra to leave but the Diamond Man insisted that they had to stay but Brian wouldn't allow it so the Diamond Man said:

No one can force me to talk to you.

He was about to leave the room when one of the agents stopped him and said:

You're not going anywhere. You're gonna stay put.

The Diamond laughed and ignored him but the agent wouldn't budge.

He said:I'm not afraid of you glassy.

The Diamond Man said: I made of Diamond not glass.

And he pushed the agent aside so the others pointed their guns at him.

Michael interfered and said:

You idiots! Who are you and where do you think you are! Put your guns away!

Ratin said: You better not mess with the Diamond Man because you'll be sorry.

Brian calmed his forces down and told them to put away their guns. He also allowed Mitra and Ratin to stay in the room.

The Diamond Man said:I don't understand where all this ignorance comes from. Do you people have to take a shot at me? Anyways, what can I do for you?

Brian said: We have been informed that an American cruise ship containing at least 2000 passengers has been robbed by pilots and we need your help to save them.

The Diamond Man asked:Where were they kidnapped?

Brian replied: Near Africa. But we don't know where the ship is now. They've deactivated all the radars on board. Are you willing to help us? The Diamond Man replied:

Help you, no! I help innocent civilians! You never would be here if you could have helped them yourselves. Do you have the ship's last coordination? What about a picture of it?

Brian brought out a map and showed the last location of the ship on it. The Diamond Man asked what it exactly was that they were asking him to do. Brian said that he need to get on a plane with them and go to the said location but the Diamond Man said that he could get there faster himself. When Brian asked how the Diamond Man replied:

I'm an alien and I can fly faster than all your jets and planes. Just give me the coordinates

Brian said: That's great! This will help you save the hostages in a shorter amount of time. Just let me contact the Navy commander General Peters.

After phoning General Peters he gave the coordinates of the location the Diamond had to fly to, to him and told him that they were expecting him on the navy ship.

They all went outdoors and everyone said good-bye to the Diamond Man, wishing him luck and he flew out of sight as they all clapped for him. The Diamond Man arrived in the area in less than twenty minutes and after getting the signal from the battleship he moved towards it. Everyone on board was waiting to greet him and the commander personal went forward, shook his hand and said:

I am honored to meet you and work with you on this project. I've seen superheroes in movies and know I have the privilege to meet one in person.

The Diamond Man thanked him and asked about their plans. The commander invited him to his personal room and showed him the previous whereabouts of the ship on the map. The Diamond Man asked:

Then you haven't found it yet.

The commander replied: Not yet but we are planning of connecting an audio transmitter and receiver to you as well as a GPS so wherever you go we can follow your whereabouts on the map. All you have to do is notify us when you find the ship and we'll take it from there.

The Diamond Man asked: Why haven't you done all this yourselves?

The commander said: We tried. We really did but it's too big of an area to cover and it takes to long to cover it all. The main problem is that the ship can't send us any signals so that makes finding it the more difficult. Even our exploration planes weren't able to find anything. When the Diamond Man asked whether they were sure that the ship was still in the waters the commander told him that they weren't sure. So, the Diamond Man asked them to prep him so he could start his mission. He flew over the waters for a while and tried to pick up the signals of the ship but no luck.

Suddenly, he had an idea. He asked the commander to give him the coordinates of the signal then he put his hands up in the form of a stop sign and concentrated on them for a while. Some blue signs showed up on his hand. He took a spin and a bunch of coordination appeared on his hands but none of them matched the ones of the ship. He continued to do the same over and over at high speed until finally with some concentration the coordinates of the ship appeared on his hands from the right direction. He flew towards it and then remembered to notify the commander and informed him that he had found the coordinates of the ship and told him that he would notify them once he found the ship. After a couple minutes of searching, he reached a strait which was surrounded by tall mountains he flew over them and went towards the strait where he finally spotted the ship. He noticed some disturbance in the signals and informed the commander:

I am currently in the exact location of the ship but they have installed a jamming device that prevents anyone from tracking the ship. The ship is in a strait. I'll go get a close look but it seems to be empty. There are just some people on the deck but the ship is empty.

The captain informed his forces of the reason why they hadn't been able to find the ship and then he sent a couple of helicopters and fighter jets to the said location.

The Diamond Man started flying over the ship and they started shooting at him. He killed them all and started looking for the passengers when he noticed a jungle way. He heard a scream from a far so he followed it and saw a number of cottages and some armed men who were standing guard but the people were not in sight. He fired at the men and killed them all and went into one of the cottages. A number of men were rapping some of the women hostages once they laid eyes on the Diamond Man they got startled and got up and started shooting at him but it was too late and before they could show a real reaction they were all killed. The women thanked him while crying. He told them that he was there to save them all and asked where the rest of the passengers were. They said:

They took them all into the jungle. We couldn't understand what they were saying. They separated the men from the women. They handed us to these criminals and took the men and other women to other bases. They want to divide us women as prizes among themselves.

Suddenly, the guards from the other tents showed up looking for the killer of their friends. The Diamond Man heard them and said to the women:

Be quiet and I'll take care of them.

Then he went out and asked the guards:

Looking for me?

They started shooting at him and some of them ran away out of fear. The next base heard all the shooting and they sent their forces there but they were all killed by the Diamond Man. The Diamond Man then shouted out:

Come out of the cottages. I won't hurt you. I'm here to save you. Don't be scared of me.

A couple minutes later some 20 women came out of the cottages. They were scared. The Diamond Man said:

Take their guns and go to the ship and kill whoever gets in your way. He thanked everyone and they all ran towards the ship. The SWAT helicopters arrived in the strait and saw the ship. Peter contacted the Diamond Man and said:

We're here. Where are the people! I'll join you in a couple of minutes.

The Diamond Man said: They've been taken into the jungle and I've saved some of the women who were being raped. They are now armed and moving towards the ship.

Peter said: I got it. Some of the forces will go into the cottages to find the rest of the hostages.

After a couple of minutes the twenty men who had run away with guns got to the SWAT team and were saved. The planes flew over the area to identify the place and report back to their commander. The ship was now under the complete control of the SWAT team and the women were transferred inside.

The commander arrived and he increased the number of forces that were set to look for the rest of the hostages. The Diamond Man arrived in a different location and conflicted with some armed men. He killed them all and some of them ran away. He knocked down the door of some of the cottages and shot four of them dead and kicked some of them out. There were some women in the cottages who were scared. The Diamond Man calmed them down and said:

Stay where you are. I'll be back.

He went to the seven remaining cottages and killed all the armed men there and freed thirty women. He told them to take the guns and run to the ship. He informed them that the SWAT team was on their way. They all ran way. There was another station and the women heard the shootings so the armed men took thirty women in the third station and put them in a cottage, ready to fire. One of the women asked whether the shootings meant the other hostages were being killed. This turned into a discussion amongst them.

The Diamond Man got to the third base and the forces started shooting. He took the guns of two of them and threw them up into a tree and wounded the others. He crushed their guns just in time for the SWAT team to get there and arrest everyone and in the first base while the Diamond Man took control of the third base. All was calm so one of the women hostages said:

Why is it so quiet? What was all that shooting for? I'm so scared.

As she was saying this, the Diamond Man opened the door and said:

I'm here to save you all. Don't be afraid of me!

After they calmed down and realized he was there to help he pointed them towards the direction of the ship where the SWAT team was located then he flew to find the rest of the hostages. He arrived in a military base and investigated the situation but there were no hostages in sight so he hit himself to the door of the base and broke it down. The guards started shooting at him but he merely ignored them and kept on looking for the rest of the hostages. A little forward and he reached a mine where a bunch of people were working. He then saw a couple of people who came out of the basement and thought to himself:

Where are they hiding the hostages? In the basement, perhaps?

He kept on going his own business and finally created a magnetic field that threw all of the criminals back. When the men who were further back started shooting at him he shot back at them as he flew over them. They all ran away and hid behind something or other. More armed forces and armed vehicles came into the base and started shooting at the Diamond Man from behind. He hit himself to one of the cars and turned it upside down. He did the same with another and everyone kept shooting at him. He went higher and opened his arms and created a strong force that changed the direction of the bullets sending them towards the armed cars. Then he went to the basement and broke down the door and went inside. Some of the hostages were being kept there. He told them that he was there to help and asked them not to come out but assured them that everything was under control. One of the men yelled:

We wanna run away now!

The Diamond Man stopped him and said: What do you think you're doing? Stop it and don't encourage the others either. It's like a battlefield out there.

Do you wanna get killed? Sit down!

His friend came forward and took him back and said:

He's right. Sit down and we'll be free soon.

Then a couple of men came into the basement and were killed with diamond bullets. Then he asked the people to close the door and wait his return. As soon as he got out he noticed that the SWAT team had got to the base and were fighting off the kidnappers so he went to their help. The navy helicopters arrived and a whole bunch of the terrorists and armed men also appeared. The Diamond Man wondered where they were all coming from so he went to the next basement where he found four more armed men that he killed. There was a little boy there who couldn't believe that the Diamond Man was real.

He said: I always wanted to see you up close. Are you real?

The Diamond Man replied: Yes, and I'll be back to see you again. He then closed the door and left. He checked the five remaining basements and noticed that it had already been cleaned of the terrorists. He brought the hostages out. The little boy ran to the Diamond Man and said:

Can I touch your body?

The Diamond Man agreed and hugged the little boy. The little boy's father thanked the Diamond Man. The captain summoned the Diamond Man. Once he ordered the passengers to be returned to the ship he informed the Diamond Man that 30 women were missing. The Diamond Man went to find them. He found another base and noticed that the women were being kept there and armed men were making them get into military vehicles. It seemed as if they were trying to escape and they appeared to be the garrison commanders. A bunch of military cars left the base and moved towards the jungle.

The Diamond Man reported back to the commander and the SWAT team was sent into the second base along with the Diamond Man himself who ordered a full-scale attack. The people were sent to the ship. The Diamond Man met up with the run-away terrorists and sent the driver and another two with him up in the sky and stopped the car. He was lifting the tent behind the car when four of the bodyguards started shooting at him. He sent them up in the sky as well and told the scared women in the car to stay where they were so they wouldn't get hurt. One of the women recognized him and started arguing about why they had to stay put. The Diamond Man informed them of the dangers ahead and assured them that he would be back for them. He then approached the next car, killed the passengers. When he lifted the back tent he was surprised to find two others who started shooting at him. He took them each and threw them up in the air but it was too late. The other cars had heard the shootings and were ready to attack the Diamond Man. Once again he asked the women to no budge and made a wave with his hands that changed the direction of the bullets and made a new wave that scattered them away for a couple of miles. Their commander and his allies got in a car and ran away. The Diamond Man continued to attack the third and fourth cars but he only found weapons in the fourth one. The fifth and the sixth car were also carrying weaponry leading to the conclusion that all hostages had been saved. The remaining forces were still showing resistance and the Diamond Man killed them all with the weapons he got from the cars. He then contacted Peter and said:

I've saved all the hostages but their lives are still in danger. Where are you?

Peter said: We're in the second base and are fighting off the remaining terrorists but they've outnumbered us. They have tons of armories.

The Diamond Man said: The only way we can get back is if we come through that base. I can't risk the lives of all these hostages. I just hope that their militia won't come this way. I'll stay with the hostages. You send two helicopters to save them.

Peter sent the two helicopters. The Diamond Man called out for the hostages to come out of hiding and they all gathered around him and thanked him. One of them even kissed him and thanked him for saving her so she could go back to her two children. After a couple of minutes the helicopters showed up and the Diamond Man flew to greet them.

The pilot said:

There's no where we can land!

The Diamond Man said:

I'll bring the hostages up to you.

He took each of the women up two by two and with the final group set up in the helicopters they flew back to the ship.

The Diamond Man flew over the base and everyone clapped for him and he waved to them all and flew towards the military base to help the SWAT team. His timing was perfect because they were surrounded by the enemy force and had nowhere to go. So, he flew above them and created a great wave which casted a large number of them away. I took a bunch of them up in the sky and let them fall. He destroyed a bunch of them this way. He then made another wave which opened the way for the SWAT team to spread out but the militia came into action once more with their weapons and bazookas. The Diamond Man destroyed them the same way he destroyed the others, by dropping them from a height. He made the machine guns collapse by hitting himself into them. He lifted another one of the machine guns and used it to kill a bunch of the terrorists. When he ran out of ammo he went back down and killed all the terrorists one by one. A bunch of the forces were scared off and ran back into the jungle. The base was finally completely under the control of the security forces.

The Diamond Man reported that the entire area had been cleaned out. When Peter asked whether their commanders had been arrested as well the Diamond Man notified him that they had run away but Peter asked him to arrest them as well. The Diamond Man flew into the depths of the jungle and followed the tracks of the cars and reached a village. A big white house attracted his attention and when he reached above it he spotted some military cars and noticed that it was surrounded with military men carrying guns. He made himself invisible and went behind a window where he spotted five militia forces. He made himself visible and before they could do anything made a wave that hit them all to the wall. He brought some rope from one of the cars and tied them up and lifted them up and took them away. When they became conscious, one of their commanders asked where they were and was notified that they were flying above the jungle. The Diamond Man had already contacted Peter regarding the fact that the terrorist commanders had been arrested.

They reached the base after a couple of minutes and he handed the commanders in. The Diamond Man asked for permission to go back to America. Peter thanked him for his services and he flew away among everyone's applause.

Back home, Ratin and Mitra welcomed him as a hero. Mitra said how they had missed him and how worried they were about what would happen. The Diamond Man asked about the Iranian statue but he was told that nothing new had come up. Then he started to tell them all about what had gone down during the operation.

A few weeks went by and they were notified that six bodies had been transferred to Italy from Iran so the research team came back together to go back to Italy. After a couple hours of flight they arrived in Rome and were in the hotel in a matter of half an hour. That night they rested and went to the research center in the morning. Alberto welcomed them back and guided the Diamond Man to the room where the bodies were kept. He quickly went there while the others were greeted and welcomed by Alberto. The Diamond Man ran into Foad on his way who was happy to see him and hugged him and said:

I'm so happy to see you. I would like to invite you to my home. My family is dying to meet you.

The Diamond Man agreed and the others joined him and they all went towards the room. Alberto opened the door and the Diamond Man was the first to go in. The three black bodies were laid down on three separate beds. The

Diamond Man touched one and said: It's unbelievable! These aren't burnt bodies. Their bodies are made of diamonds just like mine! It's driving me crazy!

The rest of the team went forward and touched the bodies. Michael said:
Whey didn't they announce on the news that these bodies are made of glass? We're all astonished!

Alberto said: We weren't informed either. We were just told that they are burnt bodies.

Mitra and Ratin were also in shock. The Diamond Man asked: Are the others the same?

Alberto replied that they were and the Diamond Man went to the next room to see for himself. Mitra accompanied him. They both looked at the bodies and Mitra pointed out the fact that they might be female but the Diamond Man appeared to not be hearing a word she was saying.

Mitra called him a couple of times but he didn't notice. Finally, she took his hand and asked:

Are you ok? You seem distracted.

The Diamond Man apologized and said: I was trying to concentrate on remembering my past. These discoveries prove that I'm not alone and I have a past.
He then went to the next room where the diamond statue was being kept. He wondered:
Why should this be one be buried as a statue and the others buried in a spaceship?

Mitra said: I would love to answer your questions but I don't really understand what's happening. All we can do is wait for the studies to be over. They've arranged for different historians from different countries to come and joined the research team. All we can do is wait and hope.

Ratin went into the room and joined their conversation. He was as baffled as they were but as Mitra had said all they could do was wait for the results obtained by the research team. Alberto informed them that a bunch of reporters were on their way to interview them and they would get to the research center in the next two hours. They continued to talk and moved from one room to the next until Alberto informed them that the reporters had arrived.

The reporters came in. They had a lot of questions and took pictures and videos of the bodies. Alberto announced the fact that the bodies were also made of glass which surprised everyone. Alberto answered all of their questions and finally ended the press conference by saying that the fact that these bodies were made of glass had just been discovered and further research had to be done in order understand the relationship between these bodies and the statue.

News about the bodies spread throughout the world and attracted the attention of an antique and drug trafficking mob. The head of the mob, Renzo, had an inside man, Roberto, in the research center. He summoned Roberto and asked about the value of the bodies and the statue. Roberto said:

They are extremely valuable! They have been arranged to remain in Italy for now for further research. They are being kept in department A.

Renzo said: They have to be mine! They'll make me rich! By the way, what are they anyway?

Roberto replied: Six black bodies made of something like glass and a glass statue of a woman. I think transparent glass statue of the women is more valuable than the others because there's only of it.

Renzo asked: What about the people who are guarding it? Do they have the key and password necessary to enter the rooms where they are kept?

Roberto promised to gather further information by the next day and Renzo asked for their addresses as well.

That night the Diamond Man and his friends were Foad's guest. His family who had come from Libya were also there and they all warmly welcomed them. Foad's mother thanked the Diamond Man for saving them in Arabic and then kissed him. The Diamond Man thanked her and asked where the children were.

Foad said: They're upstairs waiting for my cue to come down.

The Diamond Man asked him to tell them to come down. Seven screaming children ran downstairs, running towards the Diamond Man. They hugged him and kept jumping up and down around him. Ratin and Mtira were enjoying the scene. Finally, Foad asked the kids to settle down. The Diamond Man picked one of them up and sat back on the chair. Their mother came in with a big cake and then they had dinner and the Diamond Man played hide-and-seek with them afterwards, making himself invisible so the children would find him. They all had tons of fun and then went home. In the morning, they went back to the research center

On the other hand, Roberto handed in the entire necessary information regarding the statue and the bodies to the mob. Angelo, the right-hand-man handed the address of a night guard and janitor of department A to his men who kidnapped both them of them the next day while they were on their way home and took them to an undisclosed location. They were threatened to cooperate with the mob that night in order to steal the statue and the bodies or their families would be killed.

One of the guards said: We will do no such thing and we're not scared of you!

Two hours later, the door opened and the entire family of the three hostages came in. They were extremely scared and pulled themselves together. The children ran to their fathers' arms and their wives were glad to see their husbands were alive. An hour went by like this till they were separated from each other. Given the circumstances they had no choice but to cooperate. A couple minutes later, a few men came in and studied the research center on a map and a computer. They then brought a remote control car with a cutting blade on it and taught one of the guards whose post was closer to the rooms how to use it. He was supposed to guide it through the ventilators in the roof of the room where the statue was being kept and steal it. Angelo came in with a mask on his face. The guard in question said:

Since the room were the glass statue is kept is further away, my job is trickier. The ventilators are all placed in the roof above that room and cutting them could be dangerous.

Angelo shouted: I'm the one who decides what and where to cut and what to steal. That statue is unique and far more valuable than the others. If you're trying to double-cross us it won't go down very well for your family.

The guard said that he wasn't lying but Angelo just pointed out the fact that this meant they had to be more careful. Before the night shift was about to start they connected cameras, sound recorders, and a head set to each guard as well as the janitor. Angelo once again repeated his threats regarding how their families would be killed if anything fishy goes down. The second guard who was really scared begged his friends to keep their cool and not endanger his or their own families. The cutting remote control car was placed in the first guard's car trunk and the other stuff was placed in another car. They were blindfolded and their eyes were opened once they were nearby the research center. The mob members left them and they went to the center in their own car and carefully parked.

The mob were parked outside and had everything under surveillance. They were in contact with the three guards. They were waiting to get a chance to take all their stuff inside. The janitor brought a trash can and placed everything in it, avoiding the security cameras and took them inside. He emptied everything into one of the storage rooms and hid the robot inside the ventilator and informed the guard. The first guard who was the going to drive the remote control car quietly sneaked into the storage room and went towards the ventilators and placed some stuff on the car. He slowly started moving forward. Downstairs, the janitor was washing the floor and whenever someone came close to that area he sent some kind of signal to the guard to not move a muscle. The second guard was in charge of distracting the other guards in department A. Half an hour later, they got to the roof above the room in which the glass statue was kept. Angelo ordered him to cut the roof and some noise was heard throughout the center so the janitor turned the vacuum back on to hide the noise. The guard continued but suddenly a water pipe broke and water was spreading everywhere with extreme pressure. The water spread throughout the ventilator and the roof bars. Angelo aborted the plan and told everyone to get out of there. The guard returned and placed everything in the storage room and got out of there and started walking around. The janitor continued cleaning. After an hour or so, the roof bars fell and hit a lamp which then fell on the statue and electricity was transferred to it. After a couple of minutes, the power went out but the cameras were still working. The danger alarm went off and all the armed guards ran to the center. The emergency power came on. There was water everywhere.

 After checking all the rooms they found the source of the water flood which was the main water valve. They closed it. The first guard said: I'll go see what's going on.

When he came back he informed everyone that the ceiling had collapsed because a water pipe had broken. The second guard affirmed that and no one suspected that the pipe might have been cut. They quickly hid the cut pipe and were in the clear. The statue was transferred to the same room where the others were kept and in the morning the guards went home. On the way, the mob picked them up blindfolded them and took them to their families.

When the research team got to the center they heard the news but no one could have guessed that a robbery had been planned. Paula the photographer checked the videos and noticed that the roof bars had collapsed. She noticed how when the electricity wire had hit the body of the statue it had turned blue and once the power was out the light in the statue had gone out as well. She played it over and over again till she noticed something unusual which made her put the film on slow motion and maximized its size. She had noticed that the statues right hand was moving a bit. She watched it again to make sure she wasn't mistaken but it was true. First she wanted to secretly take another 3D scan of the statue but then she decided to inform Alberto. Since the scanner had been broken due to the pipe leak, Alberto said that he would transfer the statue to a different section that night and Paula could do the scan there. They decided not to inform anyone until they had the results of the scan. They were interrupted by Paula's friend who had come to ask about what had happened the other night.

On the other hand, Renzo summoned Angelo and said that he had decided to stage an attack on the site that night. Angelo said:

Sir, it's too dangerous! There are a lot of guards guarding that place and the police would pour in, in a matter of minutes.

Renzo assured him that he had thought of everything and that they would take advantage of the guards and the janitor to help them get what they wanted. Renzo then told Angelo of how his inside men that only the two of them knew about had talked of the value of the statue and assured him that they could get updates from those men after the robbery. He even had a buyer for the statue but they had to wait for everything to cool down before they could sell it. Given that the three hostages could not have been trusted, Renzo had concocted a plan with his inside men to attack the center and informed Angelo that everything was ready for a midnight attack. The plan was to be kept confidentially between the two of them until implemented to that possible police undercover agents would not figure it out.

At midnight an explosion was heard in the suburbs which shook the Earth and attracted everyone's attention. The police investigated the matter but fifteen minutes later another explosion took place. The mayor announced a state of emergency and the police were dispatched there but fifteen minutes later another explosion took place. Despite the Diamond Man's insistence of going to see what had happened Ratin said they would find out in the morning. This was all part of Renzo's plans. He summoned Angelo and told him to start the operations and keep him updated. The two guards as well as the janitor were put into action. They all went to their lockers and took some cake out and offered it to the four front door guards as well as the others throughout the site, all of whom happily ate them all. The cakes made the eight guards in department A as well as the four guards at the front door unconscious. They were then taken to the resting area of the guards and tied them up. A trash truck containing 20 mob members who were dressed as the research center guards and had masks on poured into the building and were quietly positioned in department A when the fourth explosion was heard as well.

The Diamond Man could no longer wait and begged Ratin to let him go. He gave him permission but begged him not to do anything that would get him into trouble. The Diamond Man promised and went and helped with putting out the fire, and helped out of the rumbles.

At the research center, four of the mob members took their masks off and were stationed at the front door as guards. Guard one entered the pass code of the first room and carefully opened the door. The mob members went in to steal the three black statues and when the guard opened the second room in the same manner they noticed that the glass statue was not there. Angelo asked:

Where is the statue then?

The guard replied: I have no idea. It was right here last night.

They searched another room but still couldn't find it. Angelo was furious at the guards but they insisted that they had no idea what had happened given that they were taken as hostage that day.

The fifth bomb exploded and the Diamond Man found the explosion site and headed there. Ratin and Mitra were confused as to what was happening. Ratin suggested that they wait until the next day to find out. The Diamond Man found some people who were injured in a not so crowded area where the fifth bomb had exploded and carried them to safety.

Back at the research center the mob were busy robbing the place when three of the guards from department C who had taken a break came back and noticed that the front door guards were not the same. The mob pulled a gun on them and the driver backed out and fled the site. The other three guards started shooting and the police were informed. All the other guards who had heard the shooting came running and they all started shooting at each other. Other mob members started taking the bodies of those dead out. The mob members who had been waiting outside also came in and helped drag the guards to department B where they emptied three more bodies into their cars and fled the site but they were surrounded by police officers who killed four mob members. Some other mob members who were further away came to their rescue and helped them escape and hide in a predetermined location.

The city was in chaos and the people were terrified. The Diamond Man returned to Mitra and Ratin. On the other hand, Renzo arrived at the predetermined hidden location and went to see the statues. He then asked Angelo about the three hostages and Angelo said that as he had ordered they had shot them in the foot and left them there and their families and been set free in the middle of town. He also reported that eight of their forces had been killed and six others injured.

Ratin and Mitra asked the Diamond Man about the explosions and he pointed to the fact that it was peculiar that all explosions took place in areas that were completely unrelated to each other and inhabited by hobos and homeless people whom he had saved from the fire. They all went to the research center in the morning and noticed that it had been closed off. Michael got out and talked to the police and was able to get permission to enter. Everyone was wondering what had happened. Michael got back in the car and told them about the robbery. When they entered the center they set eyes on the dead bodies and blood that was everywhere. Once they got to the room where the burned bodies were they noticed that they were gone. Alberto arrived and told them all about what had happened and how the mob had accomplices with the research center. The three men had confessed everything and had told the police that they were in on it to help save their families. Alberto also informed them of the fact that four guards had been killed and some seven others injured but he assured them that the statue was safe due to the fact that they had moved it so they could get the room where it was displayed, repaired. Alberto informed them that this meant that the research process had to be stopped for a couple of days so they all went home and discussed the possible ways the explosions and the robbery may have been related.

Ratin was the first to suggest there was a relationship between the two given that the explosions had taken place in non-significant areas and at the same time as the robbery. The Diamond Man agreed. Michael suggested that they spend their day sightseeing and having fun and everyone agreed.

On the other side of town, the police were interrogating the two guards as well as the janitor and their families. They also arrested all antique buyers and closed off the airport and all exits so that whoever had taken the burnt bodies would not be able to leave the city.

Back at the research center Alberto asked Paula to continue her research on the statue and do the necessary scans and comparisons in order to find out what had really happened. Two days later Paula called Alberto to the research room and informed him that she was now absolutely certain that the statue's finger had moved. Alberto called Michael and told them to go back to the research center the next day.

The next day they arrived at the research center and Alberto took them to the new scan room. Alberto asked them whether they saw anything different about the statue. When none of them were able to guess he played the video of the roof collapsing and everyone saw how the statue was lit when it was hit by electricity. With several replays finally the Diamond Man was the first to notice the movement in the statue's right finger and he told the others. The slow motion video revealed it to everyone. They were all excited and astonished and couldn't stop laughing. Alberto calmed them down. Ratin said:

I always knew there was something fishy going on. But how can a glass statue move its finger?

The Diamond Man said: It's not a glass statue, it's a diamond one.

Mitra said: What if it's not a statue at all.

The Diamond Man added: That's what I'm thinking but I wasn't sure whether you'd believe me.

Roberto who was the manager of department B heard all the noise. He was one of the undercover mob members working at the research center. He went and asked Alberto what was going on. Alberto took him to the scan room, introduced him to everyone as one of the best specialists in the center and showed him the video. Roberto examined the diamond statue and said:

This is so unusual. You really think that this was a reaction to the electrical force of the wires?

Alberto said that they weren't sure and more tests had to be run on the statue to find out.

That afternoon, Roberto reported everything to Renzo. Renzo asked him to make a list of the necessary tools he needed so they could conduct some tests on the bodies they had.

The next day, everyone at the center was enthusiastically working and running tests on the statue, and Roberto did the same on the bodies in the afternoon. After setting up his equipment, he studied one of the bodies under the microscope and said:

This seems to be made of the same texture as the diamond statue but it's a bit different at the same time.

Then he connected low voltage electricity to the bodies but no reaction was seen. Although he gradually increased the voltage, it was no use. After a while he got bored and took a break. Next time, he used an even higher voltage for a couple of second. This time the statue suddenly turned red and electricity went through the body. Everyone was excited at this sight but it went out very quickly. No matter how hard they tried it didn't come back. They were all disappointed. Roberto tossed the body aside and said:

I don't know. We may have had false hope thinking these are the same as that other statue.

They decided to stop working and started drinking when they heard a scream. The body had moved a finger just like the statue. Roberto quickly looked at the statue and confirmed that it was true but no further movement was seen until a few minutes later when it moved its finger again. Everyone was horrified and moved back. Roberto started examining it again when he noticed that the eyes had turned red. It had grabbed Roberto's hand. Everyone was horrified and stepped back and a number of others drew their guns on it.

Renzo yelled: You idiots! What do you think you're doing????!!!! Put your guns away!

The body had come to life. It sat up and looked around while holding Roberto's hands. It was staring at him. There was absolute silence in the room. Roberto said:

Hello my friend. I brought you to life.

The creature repeated everything Roberto had said. Roberto asked:

Who are you?

And once again the creature repeated his exact words. Then he slowly let go of Roberto's hand and moved towards the other creatures. Roberto tried to make him understand that they couldn't move and were not alive when the black diamond man asked in English:

How is it that they can't move but I can?

Everyone was shocked to learn that the black diamond man couldn't speak Italian but was able to speak English. Roberto asked him how it was possible. The black diamond man replied:

We have special powers. When we go to sleep our ears still hear and we can learn whatever language is being spoken. That's how I learned English. Now, back to my question; why don't they move?

Roberto told him that he had come to life with electricity and when the black diamond man asked what electricity was, Roberto showed him the wires that made a spark.

 Renzo asked: What kind of creatures are you? How did you get here? Are you able to learn all sorts of languages?

The black diamond man replied: Yes, I can speak Farsi as well because that's the first language I heard.

Roberto said: Then you can easily learn Italian as well.

The black diamond man said:Yes, I can easily pick up the language. But I can't remember anything from the past. I have no idea what happened to me and why I'm here.

Roberto explained that they were found in Iran in Mount Taftan, where a space ship was found in the middle of lava but the black diamond man didn't remember anything. Roberto asked:

Then how could you remember how your memory works.

The black diamond man said:

I don't know anything about that either. I told you everything I know. Perhaps my memory is not completely blank. My friends may know more.

Roberto asked how the other five had accompanied him and what they were looking for on Earth but the black diamond man didn't remember anything.

Renzo asked: What special powers do you have?

The black diamond man replied:

I can fly.

Renzo asked: How is it that you can remember that but you don't remember anything else?

The black diamond man had no answers to this question.
The black diamond man was now speaking Italian. Renzo asked him about what he ate and the black diamond man replied that their food was made of the same material as their bodies. Roberto said:
I think you mean silica.

The black diamond man couldn't be sure if that was true.
Renzo asked the black diamond man to show them how he could fly. He slowly stepped forward and slowly lifted himself up and began to fly. Everyone was astonished at this sight. The black diamond man took a spin around the room. Renzo told Roberto to not tell the black diamond man anything about the Diamond Man then he asked how it is that Roberto knew that the black diamond man ate silica. Roberto said that his eating habits were similar to those of the Diamond Man. Then, Renzo went out and quickly asked all the forces there to leave the hall and told Angelo to remind everyone to not say a word about the Diamond Man and not a word about the fact that the black diamond man had come to life. Then he went back into the room. Roberto was talking with the black diamond man. The black diamond man asked:

What's that in your hands?

Renzo explained that they were guns and people use them to defend and protect themselves against possible enemies. He then shot some bullets to show the black diamond man how a gun worked. He then took out the bullets and explained that such bullets were what could kill people and causes a loud noise when fired. The black diamond man took the gun and asked:

How is it loaded?

Renzo put the loader back into the gun. He then taught the black diamond man how to pull the trigger. The black diamond man held the gun to the wall and started shooting. He enjoyed it very much. The forces who had heard the shooting poured in worried about what had happened. Renzo assured them that they were merely practicing. He refilled the gun and handed it back to the black diamond man. He fired some more bullets and said:

I like this gun of yours.

He was holding the gun down on his foot and he accidentally shot his foot. The bullets ricocheted off his diamond foot and spread around the room. Renzo and Roberto took shelter behind a desk. He used all the bullets.

Renzo lifted his head and asked: Are you ok?

The black diamond man replied: I'm fine.

Renzo asked: How is that possible?

He could hear the bullets ricocheting off the walls.

Renzo said: This means your body is bullet-proof.

The black diamond man asked what that meant and Renzo explained:

It means that although the bullets hit your body but they don't go through so you're bullet-proof.

The black diamond man said:

Maybe I am bullet-proof.

He then asked Renzo to refill the gun and shoot at him. Renzo refused but the black diamond man insisted so Renzo accepted and shot him in the foot. The bullet ricocheted and hit the walls. Renzo laughed and hugged him. The black diamond man asked what this hugging meant. Renzo said:

It's a simple of deep affection.

The black diamond man asked:

Does this mean you love me?

Renzo replied: Yes, big time. We saved you from people who wanted to put you behind closed glasses in a museum.

What's a museum? The black diamond man asked.

Renzo explained: It's something like this room but filled with antiques, statues, and other things which are placed in certain displaying glasses for people to see. Now tell me would you prefer to be asleep and kept in such a place or are you glad that we brought you to life?

The black diamond man said: I'm grateful for the kindness you've shown towards me and for saving me.

Renzo asked: Tell me how is it that you were dead and now you are alive?

The black diamond man replied: We weren't dead. My friends and I were merely in a deep sleep. Although my friends are still asleep, they can hear everything and understand what we're saying.

Renzo said: But when people see you like that they think you're dead especially since your bodies are made of glass and diamonds which makes believing the fact that you are alive even less plausible.

The black diamond man replied: Well, our body is of a completely nature than yours.

Roberto said: First I thought you had been burnt in lava, that would have explained the black color of your skin.

The black diamond man said: No, this is the natural color of our skin.
He approached Renzo and touched his head and asked:
What's this on your body?

Renzo replied: This is my hair.

The black diamond man said: Interesting.

Roberto asked: Sir, what now? What should we do with the other?

Renzo replied: I have some more questions that have to be answered.

Then he turned to the black diamond man and asked:
How do you defend yourselves against danger?
The black diamond man laid his hand out a fired a bunch of black diamonds out of it. The diamonds went through the wall. Renzo was super excited and kept jumping up and down. He said:
You're incredible! We have to be careful. If the security forces get their hands on you, they'll put you behind a glass in a museum.

The black diamond man said: Really? Please help us lead a normal life here on Earth. We don't want to go back to sleep or be kept in a museum.

Renzo replied: It's not that easy. We need extreme strength and money to fight off the police and the government.

The black diamond man said: You can count on our strength. We'll help you in any way possible.

Renzo asked: Does that mean you'll do anything for us, no matter what? By the way what's strength and money?

Renzo took out his wallet and took out some money showed it to him and said:
In our world this is the most valuable possession of every man. We need it to survive, eat, and defend ourselves and obtain power.

The black diamond man asked: Does that mean this money in my hand means I have power? Can it kill people like guns?

Renzo laughed and said: No. Money solves problems.

The Diamond said: I don't understand. What can these tiny pieces do that makes them so powerful that they can protect us?

Renzo replied: They help us buy food, guns, cars, and hire people who are paid.

The black diamond man asked: What do 'hire' and 'paid' mean?
Renzo called a bunch of his forces in and explained:
These guys have been hired by me. They get money to stay by my side and protect me with their guns.

The black diamond man said: Now, I understand how money gives you power. Where do you get this money?

Renzo replied: That's a good question. From banks and museums.

The black diamond man asked: You mean money is kept in banks and museums.

Renzo replied: No, museums are full of valuable antiques and if we get our hands on them we can sell them and make tons of money.
What about banks? The black diamond man asked.
Banks are a place where money is kept in large amounts.
The back diamond man said:
Well, it seems that we're gonna have to lay our hands on some money.
No need to worry about it. I'll help you get the money all you have to

do is show me where it is and I'll make you rich. Do you think we can fight off the cops?

Renzo replied: I'm not sure. It depends on your strength. The government forces are likely to out-number us and they'll hunt us down no matter where we go. I have my ways. I'll be by your side every step of the way and I'll protect you but you have to have my back. Together we can do great things.

The black diamond man said: Please wake my friends the way you woke me. Remember I'll give you anything you want but only as longs as you do the same for me.

Renzo approached the black diamond man drew his hand forward for a handshake and said:

When we humans want to make a deal or a promise to which we are loyal we shake on it. You have to promise me that you will stay faithful and we will take care of each other.

The black diamond man also drew his hand towards Renzo and said:

I promise to stay by your side and always be loyal. I will do anything you ask for because I owe you. If it weren't for you I would be a corpse in a museum.

Roberto asked:

Sir, no what?

Renzo replied:

We'll wake the rest of them. Get to work!

They started putting the equipment together. The black diamond man asked if he could touch the wires and when the wires accidentally hit his body. He let go of the wire and said:

Stop!

Renzo asked:

Why?

The black diamond man said:

When I was sleeping I remember people talking around me and referring to someone as 'the Diamond Man'. I remember him touching me. Was that real?

Renzo and Roberto exchanged looks. Then Renzo said:

I'm not sure.

Roberto said:

Yes, you heard right. The Diamond Man came to Earth before you were discovered but he's forgotten all about his past as well. He is an ally of the police and our enemy. He's helping the police find you as we speak. He's served this country greatly and the police force and the people love him. There's also a statue that is kept at the research center where it is carefully protected.

The black diamond man said: So we have a powerful enemy as well.

Roberto added: Unlike your body his is transparent like this glass.

The black diamond man said: If only I could remember my past. Now, how can we stop this Diamond Man?

Renzo replied: There's no need to worry about him. He's only one person but there are six of you.

The black diamond man said: But he has the police at his side.

Renzo replied: That's true but we are stronger than them. Don't worry about it.

Roberto said: It's interesting how the electrical charge helped you retrieve your memories. This can be used to our advantage.

Renzo ordered them to help wake the other five statues. So, they connected the electrical wires to them as well and waited to see the reaction.
Renzo said:

I'm so excited. I've never had such powerful men on my side. Now, I can achieve anything I want.
The black diamond man suddenly said:
I'm hungry. I need to recharge.
Roberto said: I'll prepare silica for you as fast as possible.

He then took out his cell phone and called one of his friends to order a ton of silica. He then turned to the black diamond man and said:

It'll be here soon.

The black diamond man looked at Roberto's hands and asked: What were you talking with?

Roberto laughed and explained: This is called a cell phone. It's commonly used amongst humans.

He then showed the black diamond man his phone. The black diamond man said:

Interesting!

As they were talking one of the black diamond man's friends woke up and everyone went towards him. The black diamond man explained everything to his friend. One by one they each woke up and were not startled given that they could see their friends who had also awaken. They were able to easily talk to the mob. Roberto's phone rang to notify him that the silica he had ordered had arrived. He asked one of the men to go to the address and get it. Half an hour later the silica arrived and all six took some and started eating with a lot of noise. Everyone stared at them with astonishment. After a while, Renzo turned to the black diamond man and asked:

Did you obtain enough energy? The black diamond man replied:

Yes.

Roberto continued: What an interesting group! Two women and four men make one big strong group.

Renzo said: I can't really distinguish you from one another. What are your names?

None of them remembered what they were called so Renzo decided to give them names himself.

Renzo named the black diamond man Luca and made him the leader of the group and decided to call the rest by numbers since they appeared to be as

Twins. He turned to one and said: You're number two and each woman will be five and six.

They all liked the fact that they had numerical names and started calling each other with them.

Renzo called out to one of them and said: Number six come here.

The black diamond women went forward. Renzo continued:
Good! That's how I'll tell you apart from now on. Luca are you ready to study the map?
Luca said:

Yes we are ready to help you obtain any type of money that will give you strength and protect us.

Renzo brought a map out and gave the necessary explanations to all of them.

The next morning Roberto went back to the research center to continue his studies on the statue. No one knew what was planned in the stars for that day. Angelo brought some clothes for the black creatures. They stood in front of the mirrors and enjoyed their new clothes but Renzo believed they would be scarier without them so he ordered them to take it off. He then said to Luca:

You go first and get rid of the armed guards and we'll pour in with our guns afterwards. If you see any cops you get rid of them, get in the car and run away.

Luca replied: We got it!

They all got into the cars moved towards the bank. One of the mob members went into the bank to investigate the situation and reported back to Renzo:

All is calm. There are two armed guards inside.

Renzo ordered: Forces numbers one to six get in!

They all started to move and whoever saw them was terrified and ran away. They got into the bank and the front door guard drew his weapon on them and yelled:

Stop! Who are you?! Where do you think you're going?!

They merely ignored him and moved on but he started shooting at them. At this moment, Luca threw two of his black diamond bullets and killed the cop. Everyone in the bank was screaming. The city police started shooting at them but they were bullet-proof and felt no harm. They killed the Rome city officers

as well. Luca used the microphone that he had to contact Renzo and said:

There are no more cops! You can come in!

The mob poured in and everyone was terrified. Renzo shot off the door and left some of his forces behind it to keep an eye out for the police. They then pointed their guns towards the hostages and threatened to kill the bank manager if they didn't cooperate. But the bank manager had already rung the danger alarm. When one of the mob members figured this out and he notified

Renzo. Renzo said: It's okay. We have more power over them.

Since the bank manager had already notified the police he wasn't really that worried about the situation and easily opened the safe. The cops arrived and surrounded the place so Renzo ordered the four creatures to go out and take care of them.

He said: One, two, three, and four go out and kill them all! We'll join you when we're done here!

The four space creatures went out. The cops were terrified and asked them to surrender. They thought that they were robbers in disguise. They started moving towards the police officers and the chief police ordered his forces to shoot but they weren't harmed. Then the four creatures started shooting the police and injured a bunch of them. The chief police ordered a retreat and asked for reinforcements. They kept shooting from afar but no use. Luca told

Renzo: All clear!

A bunch of cars arrived and they all got in and were able to get away with the help of the black creatures. Then the creatures flew up and followed the cars. Everyone was startled at the scene and they figured it out that they are not human and extremely dangerous.

The chief of police reported: We thought they were in black disguise which made us think they were humans but once they started flying we understood that they weren't.

The mob parked a couple blocks away from the next bank they intended to rob and two of them went in to make sure the bank manager didn't ring the danger bell and then the black creatures entered. They killed three guards and started gathering the money before the police arrived.

Renzo said: Go out six by six and clean up the place!

They all went out and the cops started shooting at them. Luca said: Fly up and shoot them all!

The cops were surprised and a bunch of them were killed after a while. Luca and his friends helped the mob escape one more time.

A couple minutes later, they arrived at the museum. They killed the museum guards and stole a bunch of antiques. The cops got there and engaged with them but after a couple of minutes their creature friends helped them run away. The creatures flew over the mob cars protecting them from the cops and clearing their way. They were finally able to get rid of the cops and reached a safe spot.

Renzo thanked everyone and asked: How many men did we lose?

One of the mob members said: Five dead and three injured.

Renzo ordered: Go to the hospital and kill them all.

The news of these attacks spread throughout town until it reached the research center. The TV was showing the bank and museum attacks and images of the black creatures. The research team was shocked at the news and none of them believed their eyes. The Diamond Man said: I can't believe it. How have they come to life?

Roberto, who was also among them, pretended to be as surprised and astonished as the others seemed to be.

Alberto said: I can't believe it either. Does this mean that they weren't statues? They were made of diamonds!

Michael said: Believe it or not it is what it is. What we do know is that their space ship got stuck in some lava and we don't know when they came to Earth or when they got stuck in the ancient Iranian city but now they're alive and no one can stop them. There are six of them and as you can see they are bullet-proof. Look at what a mess they made today! A lot of people were killed! We have to stop them!

The Diamond Man said: Let's try to bring the statue to life.
Everyone agreed after a bit of discussion but Roberto, who was the mob's inside man, disagreed and said:
What if we damage it in any way?
Alberto agreed with the tests to be carried on and finally it was decided; they were going to bring the statue to life. They prepared the necessary equipment; a shock machine and some electrical wires.

Alberto suggested: Let's start with a weak wave of electricity to avoid high danger.
They started by injecting low voltage electricity but witnessed no effect.

Roberto said: I'm not gonna be a part of this. I don't wanna be the one who damages this statue. I'll go back to my department. Keep me updated if anything new goes down.

He went back to his room and called Renzo and told all about what was going around at the research center. Renzo said:
That would be interesting but still we outnumber them. By the way have you seen the news? What are people saying?

Roberto replied: Yes sir I saw everything. No one believed that they had come back to life. Everyone was wondering how the mob had brought the so-called statues to life. I'll let you know if they succeed in bringing the statue to life. We have to be careful. The police are no longer our only enemies.

Renzo said: No worries. I'm on it like a hawk! Investigate the matter and keep me updated.
In department A, the team was working on the diamond statue. Alberto said:
It doesn't seem to be working. We have to increase the voltage.
Everyone agreed and they set the voltage on 200 volts and connected it to the statue. Suddenly, its body turned bright blue and everyone was happy. They reconnected the electricity and this time the statue moved its finger. Everyone started screaming and jumping up and down.

The Diamond Man said: I'm certain that it's like me.

The reconnected the electricity but the statue didn't light up this time. They waited for a couple of minutes and did it again but there were no signs of movement throughout its body. They were all worried and no one spoke until

Michael said: Maybe we had false hope. Let's connect it one last time. They did so but nothing. They had all lost hop when the Diamond Man went to the statue, stood above it and said:

Wake up! You have to wake up! How can you be a mere statue and move your hands? Wake up!

Ratin took the Diamond Man's hand and said:

Calm down. It may look like you but not come to life like you did.

The Diamond Man said: No, I'm sure it's exactly like me!

Mitra suggested that they all think of other ways to wake the statue up. The

Diamond Man added: How is it that the mob could have brought those statues to life in just a matter of days and we can't do the same despite all of our facilities? I wish we could ask them.

Michael said:It would have been great if we could have asked them.

Alberto suggested:

Maybe we're going about all this wrong! Maybe they used something other than electricity to bring those statues to life!

Ratin said:

But it's been proven to us that the statue reacts to electricity.

Alberto said:

We all need to calm down. Let's suppose that this statue can come to life just like the others! We have to think positively! Let's get rid of all this negativity! Ok?

Everyone yelled: OK!

Alberto continued: Now that's more like it! Now we can see and think more clearly! Let's focus on getting the job done!

They all went for a cup of coffee. They each had their own thoughts as they were sipping their coffee.

On the other hand, the mob was putting the stolen money into packages and checking the antiques. Luca said:

Happy now? Did we do good today?

Renzo replied:Yes, very! You were able to scare all the people off and make them panic. We'll use that to our advantage from now on so we can get what we want! You proved how strong you are today!

Angelo said: Sir, did you see how they flew around and destroyed each police car one by one and opened the way for us?!

Renzo said: Yes, we're a strong team! Now you guys go and rest.

Luca said: We need food. We have to eat every day just like you or we'll lose our energy!

Renzo ordered for silica to be made for them and said to Luca:

We have another operation coming up for tomorrow. I'll go make the necessary arrangements. I'll be back in the evening.

He left the place to Angelo and left.

Back at the research center, an hour had gone by and they were still discussing ways to bring the statue to life when the Diamond Man was the first to notice that the statue's foot moved. He screamed and said:

Guys, it moved its legs!

Everyone gathered around the statue. A few minutes went by and again no reaction was seen. The Diamond Man said:

See, it's finally showing a reaction.

They were all happy and at the same time worried because they weren't sure what was happening. Alberto said:

I hope it does wake up.

The Diamond Man said to the statue:

Wake up!

And he started moving the statue's body.

Ratin tried to calm him down but suddenly the statue opened its eye. It started looking around with its big blue eyes. Everyone moved back a little and the Diamond Man was the only one who stayed put. He took the statues hand and said:

I'm glad you're awake. Welcome! Let me help you get down from that bed.

Everyone was filled with joy and they all jumped up and down and hugged each other. All that noise spread throughout the center and Roberto came into the room and saw how the statue was sitting up. He was shocked and said:

I'm glad you succeeded!

He approached the statue and said:

It looks exactly like the Diamond Man! I'm glad you finally found someone like yourself! You're not alone anymore! I'll go inform the others.

He left the room quickly. Everyone was happy. The Diamond Man said:

I'm so excited I don't know what to say!

Mitra said: Neither do I!

The diamond woman turned to Mitra and said:

I know you from somewhere. You look so familiar.

Then she turned to Ratin and continued:

And so do you! I know you two from somewhere and I have a good feeling towards you. Your skin color and body smell and your face all look so familiar.

The Diamond Man said:

It's because your body is showing a reaction to the place from which you came which is their hometown.

The diamond woman started speaking Farsi and said:

Thank you for taking care of me for all these years.

Mitra replied in Farsi: And we're glad to meet such an extraordinary being!

Alberto asked for a translation which was given by the Diamond Man. Alberto then said:

You're lucky that the first language they speak is Farsi. I wish I was an Iranian.

Everyone laughed and the diamond woman said:

I remember being unconscious and then everyone thought I was dead so they buried me. All I remember are the voices around me and then there was a silence.

Ratin said: The silence probably started when they put you in the grave.

The diamond woman said:

Yes. That's right. Ratin asked:

How did they make you unconscious?

The diamond woman replied:

I don't really remember.

Alberto asked: How is it that you can speak our language?

The diamond woman said:

It's not that I was dead. I was just asleep so my brain and my ears were still working. I can speak Farsi, English, and Italian. I am very talented in learning languages.

The Diamond Man said: Just like me! I was able to learn English very easily in the space station.

In the meantime, Roberto contacted Renzo and told him everything. Renzo said:

That means the Diamond Man is no longer alone and has help. Why don't we try them out? We have to take advantage of our new forces and build a huge empire which encompasses all other mob gangs. I've always dreamed of this day when I would be the godfather. That day is not far out thanks to my space friends. I'll make the necessary arrangements for tomorrow. Tomorrow we'll cause chaos everywhere and we'll see what this Diamond Man can do with the help of his friends. Let me know if anything changes.

Back at the research center, all the employees had come to see the diamond woman. It was an unbelievable occurrence for everybody. Two hours later some security forces came and one of them said:

The government of Italy will take full responsibility for the safety of this statue as well as the stealing of the others and we will report to Iran but right now, we have nothing to say. Now, this statue has to stay in quarantine.

The Diamond Man said: This statue belongs to no one. She's free and can go and live wherever it wants.

The security agent replied: You are completely right. But we have to take care of it and since you brought it to life you also share responsibility for putting it in danger.

The Diamond Man asked: Then why didn't you protect this center well enough to avoid such a robbery of the six statues. Did we bring those to life or did the mob? Then you better fix it! The diamond woman is not a criminal who steals or kills, the other ones are. The ones you haven't been able to stop. You have to worry about them and leave us be. We are the only ones who can stop them not you.

The security agent said:Are you making fun of me?

The Diamond Man replied: No, my friend! I was just stating the facts. You can't stop other humans from committing crime let alone aliens. Alberto interfered and tried to calm them all down. The security forces warned them that they cannot take the diamond woman out of the city

and Alberto took full responsibility for whatever was to happen to it.
The security forces finally left and Alberto turned to everyone and said:
My dear friends! We have to be really careful here. We can't just take
her anywhere we want. She's not like the Diamond Man so we have to
be more careful regarding how we conduct ourselves so we don't get
into trouble.

They decided to take the diamond woman outside and show her the
view of the city.

They also went to see the museum and banks that had been robbed that
morning. They showed her everything and the Diamond Man shared all
his memories with her. At night, they all went home but the Diamond
man and the diamond woman spent the entire night talking and
watching TV. The Diamond Man explained to her how the world
works using the TV.

In the morning, Renzo went to the hiding place and said:
Guys! We will attack three banks today. Two of the aliens along with
ten of my men will make separate teams and we'll surge the attack.

The groups were given the maps and they each went towards the
respective bank they had to rob.

Per request of the Diamond Man, the American team also went to the
city and wandered around.

Ratin asked: Happy now? We've been wandering around for a while.
The Diamond Man replied:

Yes, I have a gut feeling that there are gonna be more robberies today and we can stop them this time!

Ratin said: I hope you're not right because I don't like to see innocent people get killed.

Alberto had talked with the police and the cops were going to notify the team if another bank robbery took place so the Diamond man and woman could help. Half an hour after they had gone out, Alberto called Ratin and informed him that a robbery had taken place and he gave them the address which they put into their GPS. They went there as fast as possible but near the building there was a lot of traffic. The Diamond Man said:
I'll get out and you meet me with the car once you get there.

The diamond woman said: I know how to defend myself.
So Ratin suggested that the Diamond Man take her with him. They both got out and caused a stir among people who started filming them with their phones. The Diamond Man asked her:
Are you ready?

She replied: Yes.
He continued:
Then fly with me and we'll get there faster.

They arrived at the bank door a couple seconds later and noticed how the SWAT team had surrounded the place. They landed and everyone was happy to see them. The Diamond Man asked the SWAT team to move back and he went to open the door but since it was locked he had to use strong wave which opened it and then they went in. The robbers were gathering the money when they were surprised with the Diamond Man and woman's arrival. The black creatures were surprised to see the texture of the Diamond Man and woman's bodies. The black diamond man number 3 asked:

Who are you? You look like us but unlike us you are transparent!

The Diamond Man replied: Unlike you we are not evil! Why are you taking innocent lives?

The black diamond man number 3 replied:

We can do anything we want! Why don't you join us?! Otherwise, we'll have to kill you!

The Diamond Man said:

That wouldn't be wise at all! Surrender!

The black diamond man number 3 said:

NEVER!

And he started shooting at the Diamond Man. Bits and pieces of his body fell off because of the shootings so he started shooting at them as well. But what was interesting was the fact that when the Diamond Man started shooting the black aliens' bodies was more severely damaged than his own. They were not only wounded but had also become weak. The Diamond Man created a big wave force and hit them to the wall with it. The mob members were running away when the diamond woman flew over them taking each and throwing him aside. Numbers 3 and 4 attacked the Diamond Man and woman. They would each throw the other aside and the Diamond Man hit one of them to the window of the bank which made the window break. That one fell on a police car and the SWAT team started shooting at it. It got up and started shooting at the police.

At the same time, the black diamond man number 4 was punching the diamond woman and she couldn't get him off of her. The Diamond Man went to her rescue and threw that black diamond man out of the bank and then followed it out themselves. The two black creatures said to each other:
They're stronger than us! We have to make them move towards the rest of the group!

They started to fly and so did the Diamond Man and woman right behind them. The Diamond Man said:
We have to catch them!
So, he quickly flew towards one of them and pushed him through the windows of a nearby apartment and then dragged him down. They were breaking the glasses and punching each other when the black diamond man finally got a hold of him and smashed him into a nearby building. The Diamond Man fell to the floor.

The black diamond man then went to get the diamond woman while the other one had reached the second bank. The diamond woman followed him into the bank where she was surprised to face three black diamond men. They attacked her and threw her out of the bank but the Diamond Man arrived just in time. He started attacking all three creatures when the fourth one arrived as well. The Diamond Man was stuck! He tried to concentrate and focus. Then he created a big wave which threw all four to the sky. Then he quickly ran to the diamond woman's side and picked her up. They flew up and built a wave bubble that would not allow anyone to come close to them as well as deflecting the bullets. The four others ran away.

On the way to the third bank they once again faced the Diamond man and woman. But they were able to get to the third bank and join their friends making the total of the black diamond men six. The Diamond Man and woman got to them. Luca stood in front of the Diamond Man and woman and said:

Now, what are you going to do? There are six of us and only two of you. Let's go!

The Diamond Man laughed and starting shooting at them with the help of the diamond woman. They all spread out and started shooting back. Then they attacked the Diamond Man and woman, head on. They hit each other to the walls. Three of them picked the Diamond Man up and hit him to the ground and started beating him up!

The diamond woman was able to run away from them and went to the phone booth. She took it out of the ground and threw it at them and was able to save the Diamond Man. He was dizzy and could barely get up. The diamond woman kept shooting at the others and after a couple of second the Diamond Man regained his strength and made a wave which sent all of the aliens scattering about. Luca asked his friends:

Where does he get the strength to create such waves? Why can't we do the same?

Suddenly, the Diamond Man and woman started shooting at them and were able to injure a bunch of them. They started shooting back. The Diamond Man asked the diamond woman to hide behind him and he was able to contain them by creating one wave after another. The Diamond Man was glad to see that he was stronger than them. The black aliens were exhausted and scared. Luca said:

We have to run away! Be prepared otherwise we'll be dead meat!

The Diamond Man stopped the waves and said:

Surrender!

Suddenly, the six black aliens started shooting at them and injured both and then ran away. The SWAT team also shot at them but they were bullet-proof and were able to fly far away. The Diamond Man and woman pulled themselves together and tried to get up. After concentrating for a bit they were able to heal themselves and go back to the SWAT team.

On the other hand, the city was in chaos. A lot of buildings had been damaged and some people were hurt as well. The firefighters were busy putting out the burning cars and buildings. The Diamond man said to the diamond woman:

What a disaster!

She replied: Yes! People have been hurt for no reason. We have to arrest those guys or they'll go on doing whatever they want. Let's go find everybody else!

They then flew to their friends. Ratin was looking at the wreckage when they arrived. He said:

How'd it go?

The Diamond Man said: Not very well. They were a strong team. They shot us and then fled.

Ratin asked: Are you guys ok?

He was specifically asking the diamond woman. She replied:

I'm fine. Now I know my boundaries and how powerful I can be. I can make waves like he does.

The Diamond Man said:Really?! You can?!!!

The diamond woman said: Yes, I concentrated and was able to do it.

The Diamond Man replied: That's great! Now our powers combined can make a powerful source! We have to find those guys.

Michael arrived and said: That's enough for today! We have to go back. The city is in chaos.

They all got into their cars and went back to their lodges. Ratin said to Mitra:
Our boy is not alone anymore! Looks like he's enjoying himself!

Mitra said:Quiet down! They might hear us!
Ratin replied: I'm just saying. He's found his mate. He's not alone anymore. They're gonna have a bunch of happy days ahead of them. We have to leave them alone more often.

Mitra laughed and said: Cut it out! Don't be silly!
They both laughed and carried on with their conversation.

The diamond woman asked: What's so funny?

Mitra said: Nothing to worry about.
Then Mitra and Ratin laughed again.
On the other hand, the black diamond men and the mob members who had succeeded in robbing some money went back to their hiding place and reported back to Renzo.

He said:

The city was in great chaos today! Good job! We have now become a notorious gang that terrifies everyone. My dreams are coming true! More power to you guys!

Luca said:

We need food to help rebuild our bodies.

Renzo opened a cabinet and handed them plate full of silicon and said:

Help yourselves!

After having eaten their food, they all quietly sat in a corner and waited for the wounds to heal.

Renzo said: Guys I have a great plan to attack the section of a bank where all the gold bullions and money is kept. Then we'll head out of Italy. I have arranged for a ship at port Civitavecchia to take us. Italy is no longer a safe place for us. I have big plans. We will be joining my friends in Latin America. We'll set up a great worldwide trade there. I will be the sole trade power of

Latin America! Everyone on board?

Luca said:

I don't wanna have to fight with that diamond man and woman again.

Luca said:

No need to worry about them. After we get our hands on all that money we'll be out of here in on time. All we have to do is follow the plan.

Then they were all briefed as to what the plan entails and were ready to move.

Renzo said: I'll see you all back here in a bit and then we'll set sail. Everything's ready. Now you can go.

The city was still in shock over what had happened that day and nobody expected a second attack to take place. They got to the bank in a matter of twenty minutes. There were a number of armed forces guarding the door. Angelo ordered the forces to start the robbery. A couple minutes later two huge trucks arrived at the scene and the first one went into the building and exploded, killing a bunch of people. After the explosion, the car containing the mobsters moved to the front door and everyone got out and poured into the bank. They used some bombs they had brought along to explode the safe. They put together all the hostages who were still alive. Then they took the bank manager and ten employees, put them in a corner of the bank and tied them up to a bomb. They imprisoned the rest of the hostages in a room and warned them that if they didn't give him the code to the safe, they would all blow up. The bank manager said:

The safe is explosion-proof.

One of the mobsters replied: It's ok. I'll blow up the wall surrounding it if I have to.

The bank manager replied: No matter what you do, you won't get the code from us!

The mobster said: Are you sure?

Then he took one of the employees and stuck him with a bomb to the wall and told the others to get out of the way. He asked for the code one more time but the bank manager still refused. The mobster exploded that hostage and everyone screamed and was in shock. The bank manager said:

I can't believe you actually killed him. Please don't hurt the others.

The mobster said:

I'm not kidding around. You either give me the code to the safe or join your friend in the afterlife!

The people outside who had heard the explosions were worried. One of the woman employees begged the bank manager to give the code to them so they wouldn't hurt more people. The bank manager finally gave in. Once they had the code, opening the safe was a piece of cake. They took all the money then stuffed the hostages into the safe, shot the lock with a gun so no one could open it from the outside and were about to leave.

On the other hand, the diamond man and woman, who had heard the explosions, arrived at the site after getting the necessary permissions from the authorities. The bank was surrounded by the police. Suddenly, a car bomb exploded which killed a bunch of police officers and injured some others. The chief of police ordered a retreat. He reported: This place is no longer safe.

The black diamond men were guarding the doors to prevent anyone from getting in. Everyone was worried about what was going on in the inside and how the hostages were holding up. When the diamond man and woman got to the bank the place was filled with smoke. The chief of police told them:

The black creatures have attacked and are inside.

As he was explaining the situation another car bomb went off and some police officers were injured.

The chief commander said:

This place is not safe. We have no control over anything. Another bomb might go off any minute. We don't really know what they're up to. They have concocted a big plan for this but we don't know what it is.

One of the officers came up to the chief and said:

Sir, should we raid the place?

The chief replied:

No, they are still inside and they have a bunch of hostages. We have to wait.

The Diamond Man said:

We'll go in and fight them off.

The chief said:

That's too dangerous. We could end up endangering the lives of the hostages.

The Diamond Man said: What else can we do? Should we just sit around and wait for a miracle? Leave them to us! We know how to stop those aliens. We know how they operate.

The chief of police said:

Then just wait a couple of minutes and if nothing changes then you can go inside.

A couple of minutes later another car bomb went off which injured a large group of people. Everyone was in shock. Just as they were trying to recover from this explosion another one was heard from the inside. The chief of police said:

You can go in.

The diamond man and woman cautiously entered the bank. Took a few steps forwards when they faced someone who said:

Stop right where you are or else I'll shoot.

They ignored it and moved forward but suddenly the black aliens started shooting at them so they each had to hid behind one of the bank columns. The bank was filled with smoke and ashes. They moved a couple steps forward where they could see the black creatures. They started shooting them again injuring both. They had to hid and pause for their bodies to repair itself.

The Diamond Man asked the diamond woman: Ready?

She nodded and they both made themselves invisible and attacked the black forces. As Luca was standing, the Diamond Man attacked him and hit him to the wall. They were shocked. They could only hear the Diamond Man say:

Catch me if you can!

They started shooting around but since they couldn't see the diamond man and woman they couldn't hurt them either. Instead the diamond man and woman were injuring them and hitting them to the wall. They tried running away but another wave prevented them from doing so and instead hit them to the wall. The same thing happened a few later when they tried to run away again. Luca said:

Guys just shoot so we can get out!

Another car explosion took place as they were attempting their escape which injured another group of police officers. The black creatures took this opportunity to spread out. The fire fountains installed in the bank started working again and made the diamond man and woman wet which made them visible again.

The black creatures could now see them no matter where they went so they started shooting at them. The diamond man and woman were shocked so all they could do was make another wave that wasn't strong enough since they had been injured. So the black creatures attacked them and started beating them up. The diamond man and woman were worn out and the others were hitting desks on their heads. Finally, Luca said:

That's enough. Let's get out of here NOW!

Then he took his microphone out and said:

Boss, it's your turn!

Then they all flew out. The second truck which was parked near the bank wall exploded and killed a bunch of people.

The Diamond Man and woman were stuck under a bunch of rumble. There was smoke and ashes everywhere. A few minutes later they pulled themselves out of the rumble.

The SWAT team was looking everywhere for the dead and the hostages. They broke down the rooms and were able to save some of the hostages but the others were stuck in the safe. One of the employees said:

The bank manager and some of the other employees are missing.

No one could have guessed what had happened or where those hostages were. Wild guesses were made regarding fate. One suggested that they had been killed and one of the SWAT members said:

The safe is locked too so there's no one there.

But suddenly he noticed the key to the safe and said:

Someone has broken the key lock to the safe.

The chief of police asked:

You mean they just wanted to mess this place up? If that's not the case then why is the safe locked? It should be open and the money gone. But no one has left this bank.

While these discussions were taking place the black creatures arrived at a parking lot where they got into a van and headed towards their hiding place.

The driver said: What a fight! I loved the explosions! They were so exciting! I wish I could have seen it up-close.

Luca said: If you were there you would have been dead by now!
They arrived at their hiding place and the money and the gold bullions arrived in four separate vans. They had blindfolded the hostages. Renzo was happy to see them all and ordered the hands and feet of the hostages to be tied up. They threw them into one of the rooms. There was a bus parked outside. Renzo said:
Go put on your new clothes and place the money and the gold in the safe and under the bus seats.

Luca asked: Sir, what kind of clothes are these?
Renzo laughed and said:
These are clothes worn by nuns. Put them on and get in the bus. Don't forget to wear the face coverings as well. No one can see your faces.
The mobsters that were accompanying Renzo were all disguised as nuns and priests. After hiding the gold and the money, they headed out. Renzo told one of his mobsters:
When you hear from me, free the hostages somewhere not so crowded.

He said: You don't want us to kill them?

Renzo replied: You idiot! If we kill them then who is going to tell the news reporters of our glorified hit and run? Now, get to work!

Back at the bank no one had the slightest clue that an actual robbery had taken place. The American research team arrived at the site and everyone was trying to put out the explosions and help save those injured. An hour later, they were finally able to fix the busted safe lock and open the safe. What they witnessed then and there astonished them. There was absolutely nothing and no one there! The SWAT captain said:

What is going on? There's no money and no gold! When did they get out? How did we miss them?

Having taken a look at the safe one of the SWAT team members noticed a hole in the back and said:

Sir, it looks like they used this hole to get out.

Some of the forces went into the hole and ended up in the sewers but it was too late. They had already fled the scene.

The SWAT captain said:

This means they have taken the hostages to help them carry the gold and the money. Their lives are endangered. If we find them we have to be careful not to put the hostages in harm's way.

The relief teams were helping those injured. The America team was helping those injured. Ratin said:

What's going on today?!!! Someone has to stop these people!

The police officers were ordered to close off all exits and keep an eye on them.

All of the mobsters were moving towards port Civitavecchia. On the way, they got to a checkpoint. One of the SWAT team members looked up and noticed that the entire bus was full of priests and nuns and a number of others are asleep.

The driver said: My friend, we're coming from the Vatican. We're missionaries who are headed to a cruise.

The SWAT team member said:

Sorry for bothering you! You can continue your way.

Renzo, who was disguised as a priest laughed inside and then they left. But the police forces had no idea that these passengers were cruel people were hiding themselves under the garments of holy beings. Finally, they arrived at the port and got on the ship and set sail towards Latin America. Renzo said:

First we'll go to Africa and rest there for a while. Then, we'll go to one of the Latin American countries. Before that I will ask one of my friends which country is the best destination for us. Whichever country gives us more money and provides better facilities will be our destination. Open the champagne! We want to celebrate!

On the other hand, everyone was looking for the mobsters and the black creatures. The people were scared and security measures were taken throughout the city. The army was called in to provide security throughout the city, but it was too late. No one knew that the storm had already blown over.

Renzo contacted his men and said:

Free the hostages tomorrow morning. Set them loose so they can tell everyone about our little stunt. They'll make us famous! Be on standby for my further commands.

Everyone in the city was talking about the black creatures and how they had come to life and all the crimes the six of them had committed. People around the world were also talking about the diamond woman and how she had come to life.

The police spent a long time investigating where the mobsters and the black creatures had gone but their findings were inconclusive. On the other hand, research on the Diamond man and woman continued in Italy with a hope to discover the secret to their past.

www.ingramcontent.com/pod-product-compliance
Lightning Source LLC
Chambersburg PA
CBHW080731250626
47170CB00011B/2899